Eve felt Talos's dark gaze fall upon her mouth as he said softly, "I'll show you the place where I first kissed you."

Her bones turned to liquid. She looked up at him, her heart pounding as she licked her lips involuntarily. "Where is that?"

His eyes were hot and dark. "In Venice."

"Venice," she repeated, and the word was a wistful sigh. She looked up at him with yearning, knowing she should refuse—knowing she should stay in London and see the specialist Dr. Bartlett had recommended. But her refusal caught in her throat. Caught by her romantic dreams. *Caught by him.*

Talos reached down to stroke her tender bottom lip with his thumb, caressing her face with his powerful hands.

"Come to Venice," he said darkly. "I will show you everything."

He cupped her face with both hands, holding her hard against his body as he looked down at her, commanding her with his gaze.

"And then," he whispered, "you will marry me."

With Valentine's Day coming up, it's the perfect opportunity to indulge in some romance, and where better than with eight new fantastic Harlequin Presents® stories!

This month we have bestselling author Lynne Graham with the second book in her PREGNANT BRIDES trilogy, *Ruthless Magnate, Convenient Wife*. Get whisked away to the stunning Moscow where ruthless billionaire Sergei Antonovich will stop at nothing to make the shy and virginal Alissa his convenient wife!

And please help us celebrate Carole Mortimer's 150th book, *The Infamous Italian's Secret Baby*. When one night leads to one baby, Bella Scott finds herself at the mercy of infamous Gabriel Danti!

Why not treat yourself with a wonderful story of blackmail in Robyn Donald's *The Rich Man's Blackmailed Mistress*. And Talos Xenakis's plans for revenge change when he discovers his mistress is pregnant in Jennie Lucas's *Bought: The Greek's Baby*.

Out this month is our first book in the BRIDE ON APPROVAL miniseries. Whether bought, sold, bargained for or bartered, these brides have no choice but to say I do. Be sure not to miss Caitlin Crews's debut book, *Pure Princess, Bartered Bride*.

Who will reunite the two Stefani diamonds, and become ruler? Find out in the last installment of THE ROYAL HOUSE OF KAREDES, *The Desert King's Housekeeper Bride* by Carol Marinelli. But the saga continues in April with DARK-HEARTED DESERT MEN. Four brooding sheikhs with a hint of Karedes in them.

And last, but by no means least, don't forget about any of our fabulous new miniseries coming out in 2010. The glamour, the excitement, the intensity just keep getting better.

Wow! 2010—this truly is the year of Presents! *Your everyday luxury.*

Jennie Lucas

BOUGHT: THE GREEK'S BABY

TORONTO • NEW YORK • LONDON
AMSTERDAM • PARIS • SYDNEY • HAMBURG
STOCKHOLM • ATHENS • TOKYO • MILAN • MADRID
PRAGUE • WARSAW • BUDAPEST • AUCKLAND

PLEASE RECYCLE • THIS PRODUCT IS RECYCLABLE

Recycling programs
for this product may
not exist in your area.

ISBN-13: 978-0-373-23659-6

BOUGHT: THE GREEK'S BABY

First North American Publication 2010.

Copyright © 2009 by Jennie Lucas.

This edition published by arrangement with Harlequin Books S.A.

® and TM are trademarks of the publisher. Trademarks indicated with ® are registered in the United States Patent and Trademark Office, the Canadian Trade Marks Office and in other countries.

www.eHarlequin.com

Printed in U.S.A.

All about the author...
Jennie Lucas

JENNIE LUCAS had a tragic beginning for any would-be writer: a very happy childhood. Her parents owned a bookstore, and she grew up surrounded by books, dreaming about faraway lands. When she was ten, her father secretly paid her a dollar for every classic novel (*Jane Eyre, War and Peace*) that she read.

At fifteen, she went to a Connecticut boarding school on scholarship. She took her first solo trip to Europe at sixteen, then put off college and traveled around the U.S., supporting herself with jobs as diverse as gas-station cashier and newspaper advertising assistant.

At twenty-two, she met the man who would be her husband. For the first time in her life, she wanted to stay in one place, as long as she could be with him. After their marriage, she graduated from Kent State University with a degree in English, and started writing books a year later.

Jennie was a finalist in the Romance Writers of America's Golden Heart contest in 2003 and won the award in 2005. A fellow 2003 finalist, Australian author Trish Morey, read Jennie's writing and told her that she should write for the Harlequin Presents® line. It seemed like too big a dream, but Jennie took a deep breath and went for it. A year later Jennie got the magical call from London that turned her into a published author.

Since then, life has been hectic—juggling a writing career, a sexy husband and two young children—but Jennie loves her crazy, chaotic life. Now if she could only figure out how to pack up her family and live in all the places she's writing about!

For more about Jennie and her books, please visit her Web site at www.jennielucas.com.

To Patty Sowell, the miracle of our house,
with gratitude

CHAPTER ONE

TALOS XENAKIS had heard a lot of lies in his life, particularly in relation to his beautiful, ruthless ex-mistress. But this one topped them all.

"It can't be true," he said in shock, staring at the doctor. "She's lying."

"I assure you, Mr. Xenakis, it's true," Dr. Bartlett replied gravely. "She has no memory. Not of you, not of me, not even of her accident yesterday. And yet there's no physical injury."

"Because she's lying!"

"She was wearing a seat belt when her head hit the air bag," Dr. Bartlett continued. "There was no concussion."

Talos stared at him with a scowl. He had a reputation as a doctor of immense skill and integrity. He was rich from a lifetime of serving wealthy, aristocratic patients—so he couldn't be bought. He was known as a family man, still completely in love with his wife of fifty years, an adored father of three and grandfather of eight—so he couldn't be seduced. So he honestly must believe Eve Craig had amnesia.

Amnesia.

Talos's lip curled. After all of her devilish cleverness, he would have expected more of her.

Eleven weeks ago, after stabbing him in the back, Eve Craig had vanished from Athens like a ghost. His men had searched for her all over the world without success until two days ago, when she'd suddenly resurfaced in London for her stepfather's funeral.

Talos had dropped a billion-dollar deal in Sydney, ordering his men to trail her until he could reach London on his private jet. Kefalas and Leonidas had been right behind Eve yesterday afternoon when she'd left the private hospital in Harley Street. They'd watched her tuck her long, glossy dark hair beneath a silk scarf, put on big black sunglasses and white driving gloves and drive away in her silver Aston Martin convertible.

Right into a red postbox on the sidewalk.

"It was so strange, boss," Kefalas had told him that morning when he'd arrived from Sydney. "She seemed fine at the funeral. But leaving the doctor's office she drove like a drunk. She didn't even recognize us when we helped her back into the hospital after the accident."

Now, Dr. Bartlett looked equally puzzled as he scratched the back of his wispy white head. "I held her overnight for observation, but cannot find anything physically wrong with her."

Talos ground his teeth. "Because she doesn't have amnesia. She's playing you for a fool!"

The elderly doctor stiffened. "I do not believe Miss Craig is lying, Mr. Xenakis. I have known her since she was fourteen, when she first came here with her mother from America." He shook his head as he mused, "All the tests came back negative. The only symptom seems to be the amnesia. Leading me to perhaps wonder if the accident was merely the catalyst—the trauma was an emotional one."

"You mean she brought it on herself?"

"I wouldn't say that exactly. But this is outside my field. It's why I've recommended a colleague, Dr. Green."

"A psychiatrist."

"Yes."

Talos latched on to the one valuable bit of information. "So if there's nothing physically wrong with her, she can leave the hospital."

The doctor hesitated. "She's certainly strong enough. But as she has no memory, perhaps it would be better if a member of her family…"

"She has no family," Talos interrupted. "Her stepfather was her only relative, and he died three days ago."

"I did hear about Mr. Craig, and was very sorry. But I hoped perhaps Eve might have an aunt or uncle, or even a cousin in Boston…"

"She does not," Talos said evenly, although he had no idea. He only knew nothing was going to keep him from taking Eve away with him today. "I am her…" *What? Ex-lover bent on revenge?* "Boyfriend," he finished smoothly. "I will take care of her."

"So your men told me yesterday, when they said you were on your way." Dr. Bartlett eyed him as if he did not quite like what he saw. "But it does not sound as if you even believe she needs special care."

"If you say she has amnesia, I have no choice but to believe it."

"You called her a liar."

Talos gave a crooked grin. "Creative untruths are part of her charm."

"So you are close?" The doctor looked up at him with narrowed eyes. "Do you plan to marry her?"

Talos knew the answer the man wanted— the only answer that would release Eve into his power. And so he told the truth. "She is everything to me. Everything."

Scrutinizing Talos's expression, the doctor stroked his beard with something like satisfaction, then nodded in a sudden brisk decision. "Very well. I'll release her into your care, Mr. Xenakis. Take good care of her. Take her home."

Take her to Mithridos? Talos would die before he would pollute his home that way. But Athens…yes. He'd lock her up and make her thoroughly regret betraying him. "You will release her to me today?"

The doctor nodded. "Yes. Make her feel

loved," he warned. "Make her feel wanted and secure."

"Loved and secure," he repeated, barely able to keep the sneer from his face.

Dr. Bartlett frowned. "Surely, Mr. Xenakis, you can appreciate what these last twenty-four hours have meant to Eve. She's had nothing to cling to. No memory of family or friends to sustain her. No sense of home or memory of belonging. She didn't even know her name until I told her."

"Don't worry," Talos said grimly. "I'll take good care of her."

But as he started to turn away, the doctor stopped him. "There is something else you should know."

"What?"

"Normally I would never disclose this information. But in this unique case, I feel the need for informed care far exceeds the concern for privacy...."

With a muttered curse in Greek, Talos tapped his foot impatiently. "What is it?"

"Eve is pregnant."

At that word, Talos's head shot up. His heart literally stopped in his chest.

"Pregnant?" he choked. "When?"

"When I did the ultrasound yesterday, I estimated conception in mid-June."

June.

For nearly all of that month Talos had barely left her side. He'd kept tabs on his business almost unwillingly, begrudging every moment of his life that wasn't spent in bed with her. Their affair had burned him through, blood and bone. He'd thought—God help him—that he could trust her. Because lust had seized his mind and will.

"I feel I'm at fault," Dr. Bartlett continued regretfully. "If I'd had any idea how upset she was at the news of her pregnancy, I would never have let her drive away from the hospital. But don't worry," he added hastily, "your baby is fine."

His baby.

Talos stared at him, hardly able to breathe.

The doctor suddenly gave a hearty, cheerful laugh, patting him on the back. "Congratulations, Mr. Xenakis. You're going to be a father."

Around her, Eve was dimly aware of a whisper of voices and the distant hum of a radiator. She felt someone—the nurse?—sweep a cool cloth against her forehead. The soft sheets against her skin felt heavy. She smelled the fresh scent of rain and cotton. But she stubbornly kept her eyes closed.

She didn't want to wake up. She didn't want to leave the dark peacefulness of sleep, the warmth of barely remembered dreams that still cradled her like an embrace.

She didn't want to return to the nothingness of existence, where she had no memories. No identity. Nothing to cling to. It was an emptiness far worse than any pain.

And then the doctor had told her three hours ago that she was pregnant.

She couldn't remember conceiving the child. Couldn't even remember the face of her baby's father. But she would meet him today. He would be here any minute.

Covering her head with her pillow, she squeezed her eyes shut. She was racked with nervousness and fear at the thought of meeting him for the first time—the father of her unborn baby!

What kind of man would he be?

She heard the door open and close. She

held her breath. Then someone sat heavily next to her, causing her body to lean toward him on the mattress. Strong arms suddenly were around her. She felt the warmth of a man's body, breathed in the woodsy musk of his cologne.

"Eve, I'm here." The man's voice was deep and low, with an exotic accent she couldn't place. "I've come for you."

A thrill rushed through her. With an intake of breath, she pushed aside the pillow.

He was so close to her. She saw the sharpness of his cheekbones first. The dark scruff on his hard jaw. The tawny color of his olive skin. Then, as he drew back, she saw his whole face.

He was, quite simply, breathtaking.

How was it possible for a man to be at once so masculine—and so beautiful? His black hair brushed the top of his ears. He had the face of an angel. Of a warrior. His Roman nose had been broken at least once, from the tiny imperfection of the angle. He had a full, sensual mouth, with a twist of his lips that revealed arrogance and perhaps more—cruelty?

His eyes gleamed down at her, dark as

night. And beneath their black depths, for a moment she saw a ravaging fire of hatred—as if he wished she were dead, as if she were a ghost he'd long ago consigned to hell.

Then she blinked, and he was smiling down at her with tender concern.

She must have imagined that fiery hatred, she thought in bewilderment. Not surprising considering how screwy her head had been since the accident—an accident she couldn't even remember!

"Eve," he whispered as he stroked her cheek. "I thought I'd never find you."

The touch of his rough fingers against her skin burned her. She felt a sizzle down her neck to her breasts, making her nipples taut and her belly spiral in a strange tightness. With an intake of breath, she searched his face, hardly able to believe the evidence of her own eyes.

This—this man was her lover? He looked nothing like she'd expected.

When Dr. Bartlett had told her that her boyfriend was on his way from Australia, she'd imagined a kind-looking man with a loving heart, a sense of humor. A gentle man who would share his troubles while they washed dishes together at the end of the day. She'd dreamed of a loving partner. An equal.

Never in her wildest dreams had she ever imagined a dark god like this, cruelly beautiful, masculine and so powerful that he could no doubt slice her heart in two with a look.

"Aren't you glad to see me?" he said in a low voice.

She searched his face, holding her breath.

But no memories rushed through her, no recollections of the hard curve of his cheek or the slightly wicked twist to his sensual lips. No memories of a thousand little intimacies between lovers. Nothing!

He helped her sit up. His hands lingered possessively on her back, causing a sudden heat across her body.

Eve licked her lips nervously.

"You are…you must be…Talos Xenakis?" she ventured, waiting for him to deny it. Almost hoping he would, and that her real boyfriend, the kind-faced man with the gentle eyes, would walk through the door.

The Greek tycoon's hands on her back paused.

"So you do recognize me."

She shook her head. "No. Your two employees…the doctor…they told me your name. They said you were on your way."

He looked down at her, searching her face.

"Dr. Bartlett told me you had amnesia. I didn't believe it. But it's true, isn't it? You really don't remember me."

She could only imagine how that must hurt him! "I'm sorry," she said, rubbing her forehead. "I keep trying, but the first thing I can remember is your employee—Kefalas?— pulling me from my car. It was a lucky thing they were in the car behind me!"

His lips seemed to curve imperceptibly. "Yes. Very lucky." He sat up straight. "You will be leaving the hospital today."

She took a deep breath. "Today?"

"Right now."

"But…" She bit her lip then blurted out, "But I still can't remember anything! I hoped when I saw you…"

"You hoped seeing me would bring your memory back?"

She nodded miserably. There was no point in feeling disappointed, she told herself fiercely, or making him feel more badly about it than he must already!

But she couldn't stop the lump in her throat. She'd been counting on the idea that when she saw the face of the man she loved, the man who loved her, her amnesia would end.

Unless they didn't love each other, she thought suddenly. Unless she'd gotten pregnant by a man who was barely more than a one-night stand.

"I'm sure you must feel so hurt," she said, trying to push away her sudden fear. She said haltingly, "I can only imagine how it must feel, to love someone who can't remember you."

Do you love me? she thought desperately, trying to read his face. *Do I love you?*

"Shhh. It's all right." Lowering his head, he kissed her tenderly on the forehead. The warmth of his nearness was like the summer sun on a winter's day. Then he lifted her chin, and his dark eyes whipped through her like a blast of heat. "Don't worry, Eve. In time, you will remember—everything."

Looking into his face gratefully, Eve realized that her first impression of him had been utterly wrong. He wasn't cruel. He was kind. How else to explain the fact that he could be so gentle and patient and loving, pushing aside his own hurt to focus only on her?

She took a deep breath. She would be as brave as he was. Pushing the blankets aside, she said over the lump in her throat, "I'll get dressed to go."

He stopped her. "Wait. There's something else we need to talk about."

She knew instantly what he meant to discuss. And without the barrier of blankets between them, in just her paper-thin hospital gown, she felt painfully bare, vulnerable in every way. She yanked the blankets back over her body, tugging them halfway to her neck.

"He told you, didn't he?" she whispered.

His voice was low, almost grim. "Yes."

"Are you happy?" Her voice trembled. "About the news?"

She held her breath as his darkly handsome face stared down at her. When he finally spoke, his voice was charged with some emotion she didn't recognize.

"I was surprised."

She searched his gaze. "So the baby wasn't something we planned?"

His hands tightened, twisting the blanket in his grip. He glanced down at it, then looked at her.

"I've never seen you like this," he said in a low voice. His black gaze hungrily caressed her face. With his fingertips, he brushed some dark tendrils from her cheek. "No makeup. Bare."

She tried to pull away. "I'm sure I look terrible."

But he drew her closer. His eyes were dark as he looked down at her, making her shiver from deep within.

"Are you happy about the baby?" she said softly.

He put his arms around her. "I'm going to take good care of you."

Why wouldn't he answer? She swallowed, then lifted her head to give him a weak smile. "Don't worry, I'm not an invalid. I hope the amnesia will disappear in a day or two. Dr. Bartlett said something about a specialist—"

His arms tightened around her, cradling her against his hard chest.

"You don't need another doctor," he said roughly. "You just need to come home with me."

She could feel the beat of his heart against

her cheek through his black button-down shirt. She was enveloped in his masculine scent, sandalwood and amber, exotic and woodsy. Against her will, she closed her eyes. She breathed in his smell, heard the beat of his heart, felt his warmth.

Everything else faded. The private hospital room, the nurses and doctor visible through the window of the door, the sound of one of Talos's men speaking urgently into his cell phone in some language she didn't recognize, the antiseptic smell, the beeps of the machines…it all faded.

There was only this.

Only him.

Held securely in his strong arms, for the first time since her accident she felt safe and loved. She felt as if she had a place in the world. With him.

He kissed her hair softly. She felt the warmth of his breath, the hot caress of his lips, and a tremble went over her. Fear? Longing?

Did he love her?

She reached upward, cupping his rough jawline with her hands. Though his clothes were sharply pressed, the dark shadow on his chin suggested he'd changed clothes on the plane without bothering to shave. He'd rushed here from Australia. He'd flown all night.

Did that mean love?

"Why didn't you come to London with me for my stepfather's funeral?" she said slowly.

He paused. When he spoke, he seemed to choose his words with care.

"I was busy in Sydney acquiring a new company. Believe me," he said, "I never wanted to be away from you for this long."

Eve felt there was something he wasn't telling her. Or was that just her own confusion playing tricks on her? She couldn't trust anything in this hazy, empty world, not even her own mind! "But why—"

"You are so beautiful, Eve," he said, cupping her face. He exhaled in a rush. "I almost feared I'd never see your face again."

"When you heard about the accident, you mean? You were worried about me?" she said in a small voice. When he didn't answer, she licked her lips. With a deep breath, she asked the question that had been burning through her. "Because we love each other?"

His jaw clenched as he took a deep breath.

"You were a virgin when I seduced you, Eve," he said in a low voice. "You'd never been with any man before I took you to my bed three months ago."

She'd been a virgin?

A wave of relief washed over her. Learning she was pregnant by a boyfriend she couldn't remember had been a tremendous shock. She'd wondered why they weren't married— wondered all sorts of things. But if Talos had been her one and only lover, if she'd been a virgin at twenty-five, surely that said something about her character?

But did it also mean love?

She looked up into his handsome face, opening her mouth to ask again, *Do I love you? Do you love me?*

Then she stopped.

There was something beneath his darkly penetrating eyes. Something he wasn't saying. Something hidden beneath his words.

But before she could understand what her intuition was telling her, Talos placed his broad hands over hers. The warmth of his fingers burned her, intertwined with her own.

Trapping her, but not against her will. Her heart pounded faster.

"Get ready to leave." He lowered his head to kiss her on the temple, running his hands up and down her bare forearms. "I want to take you home."

Her breathing became short and shallow as he touched her skin. Little prickles of sensation sped up her arms, down her back, making her hair stand on end. The tingle swirled across her earlobes, down her neck, making her naked breasts beneath her thin hospital gown suddenly feel tight and full. She tried to remember the question she'd been asking, but it had already swept from her mind.

"All right," she breathed, looking up into his handsome face.

Gallantly, he helped her from the bed, lifting her gently to her feet. She was more aware than ever of how much taller he was, how much more powerful. He was at least six inches taller, with an extra hundred pounds of pure muscle. Looking up at him, she forgot everything but her own longing and fascinated desire for the man towering over her like a dark angel.

"I'm sorry it took so long for me to reach you, Eve," he said in a low voice. "But I'm here now." He kissed her head softly, his arms tightening around her as he pulled her into an embrace. "And I'm never going to let you go."

CHAPTER TWO

BENEATH heavily lidded eyes, Talos watched Eve as he led her to the black Rolls-Royce purring on the street in front of the hospital.

She wasn't faking her amnesia. In spite of his initial incredulity, he now had no doubt. She had no idea of who he was or what she'd done.

And now she was pregnant with his child.

That changed everything.

He gently helped her to the car. She had no luggage. One of his men had taken her smashed Aston-Martin to the garage, while the other had gone to make quiet amends for the smashed postbox. She wore the black silk dress and carried the black clutch purse from her stepfather's funeral yesterday.

The black dress clung to her breasts and hips when she walked, the silk shimmering and sliding against her hips and breasts. Her dark, glossy hair had been brushed into a fresh ponytail.

She wore no makeup. It made her look different. Talos had never known her to go out without lipstick before—although God knew, with her lustrous skin, full pink lips and sparkling blue eyes, she didn't need it to cause every man she met, from the elderly hospital porter to the teenaged boy walking past them on the sidewalk, to stop and catch his breath.

And as she turned back to face him on the sidewalk with a sweetly innocent smile, Talos was grimly aware that he was far from immune to her charm.

"Where are we going?" she asked, crinkling her forehead. "You never said."

"Home," he replied, guiding her into the backseat of the limousine. He closed the door behind her.

His body's reaction to her was irritating— and troubling. He didn't like it. Because he hated her.

When he'd first seen Eve in the hospital, she'd been curled up on the single bed beneath a thick blanket. She'd looked pale and wan, nothing like the vivacious, tempestuous vixen he remembered. Sleeping, she'd looked innocent, far younger than her twenty-five years.

She'd looked small. Fragile.

Talos had come to London specifically to destroy her. For the last three months, he'd been dreaming of it.

But how could he take his revenge if she not only had no memory of her crimes, but she was pregnant with his baby?

Tightening his hands into fists, he stalked to the other side of the car. Though it was only September, summer had abruptly fled London. A steady drizzle was falling from low gray clouds.

He climbed in beside her and she turned to him without missing a beat. "Where is our home?"

"My home—" he closed his door with a bang "—is Athens."

She gaped at him. "Athens?"

"It's where I live, and I must take care of you." He gave her a brief, tight smile. "Doctor's orders."

"So I live there with you?"

"No."

"We don't live together?"

"You like to travel," he said ironically.

"So where are my clothes?" she said in a small voice. "And my passport?"

"Likely at your stepfather's estate. My staff will collect your things and meet us at the airport."

"But…" She looked out the window, then turned back to face him and said in a rush, lifting her chin, "I want to see my home. My childhood home. Where is it?"

He gave her an assessing glance. "Your stepfather's estate is in Buckinghamshire, I believe. But visiting there won't help you. You spent one night there before the funeral. It hasn't been your home for a long time."

"Please, Talos." Her sapphire eyes gleamed. "I want to see my home."

His brow furrowed as he looked down at her pleading face.

Eve really had changed, he thought. His mistress had never begged him for anything. She'd never even said *please*.

Except…

Except for the first night he'd taken her to

his bed, when all her defenses had been briefly stripped away and he'd discovered the most desired woman in the world was, against all expectations, a virgin. As he'd pushed himself inside her, she'd looked up at him in a breathless hush with those violet-blue eyes, and he'd thought…he'd almost thought…

He cut off the memory savagely.

He wouldn't think about how it had once been with her. He wouldn't think how she had nearly made him lose everything, including his mind.

Eve Craig was a fatal habit that he'd finally broken—and he intended to keep it that way.

"Very well," he ground out, turning back to face her. "I will take you home—but just to collect your things. We cannot stay."

Her lovely face brightened. She looked so young without makeup, with her hair in the casual ponytail. She looked barely old enough to be in college, far younger than his own thirty-eight years.

"Thank you," she said warmly.

Thank you. Another phrase he'd never heard from her before.

He turned away, leaning back in the beige

leather seat as his chauffeur drove smoothly through the city, turning right from Marylebone to the Edgware Road. As the car merged onto the M1 heading north, Talos stared out at the passing rain, then closed his eyes, tense and weary from jet lag and the whiplash of the past two days.

Eve, pregnant.

He was still reeling.

No wonder she'd crashed her car, he thought dully. Just the thought of losing her figure and not fitting into all her designer clothes must have made her crazy. All those months of not being able to drink champagne and dance till dawn with all of her rich, beautiful, shallow friends? Eve must have been more than shocked—she must have been furious.

Eve, pregnant.

He would not trust her to take care of a house plant, much less a child. She was not even slightly maternal. She wouldn't love a baby. She was the least loving person Talos had ever met.

Slowly, he opened his eyes.

He hadn't even known about the baby an

hour ago, but now he was absolutely sure of one thing.

He had to protect his child.

"So I don't live in England," he heard her say. Steeling his expression, he turned to face her. Her face looked bewildered, almost sad as she added hesitantly, "I don't have a home?"

Home. Against his will, he had the sudden image of Eve in his bedroom at Mithridos, spread across his large bed, with the curtains twisting from the sea breeze coming off the sparkling Aegean. That had never happened, and it never would!

"You live in hotels," he answered coldly. "I told you. You travel constantly."

"So how do I hold down a job?" she said in disbelief.

"You don't. You spend your days shopping and attending parties around the world. You're an heiress. A famous beauty."

She gaped at him. "You're joking."

"No." He left it at that. He could hardly explain how she and her dissolute friends traveled in packs like parasites, sucking a luxury hotel dry before moving on to the next. If he told her that, she might hear the scorn in his voice and question the true nature of his feelings.

Malakas, how was it possible that he'd been so caught by her? What madness had possessed him to be so enslaved?

How could he make sure that his child never was neglected, hurt or abandoned by her after she regained her memory?

A new thought suddenly occurred to him.

If she could not remember him, if she could not remember who she was or what she'd done, it meant she would have no idea of what was about to hit her. She would have no defenses.

A slow smile curved his lips as he built his new plan. He could take everything from her, including their baby. And she would never see it coming.

"So I was here for my stepfather's funeral," she said softly. "But I'm not British."

"Your mother was, I believe. You both returned to England some years ago."

She brightened. "My mother!"

"Dead," he informed her brutally.

She froze, her face crumpling. Watching the swift movement of scenery on the outskirts of London through the window behind her, he remembered that her mother's death was fresh news to her. And that he was supposed to be in love with her. He had to make her believe that if he wanted his plan to succeed.

"I'm sorry, Eve," he said abruptly. "But as far as I know, you have no family."

"Oh," she said in a small voice.

Pulling her into his arms, he held her close against his chest, kissing the top of her head. Her hair, messy and unwashed, still managed to smell like vanilla and sugar, the scents he associated with her. The scent that immediately made his body go hard and taut with longing, with the immediate temptation of a long-desired vice.

Thee mou. Why couldn't he stop wanting her? After everything she'd done, the way she'd nearly ruined him, how was it possible that his body still longed for her like a dying man thirsting for water? Was he really such a suicidal fool? Did he have no honor, no pride?

He had pride, he thought, clenching his jaw. It was *her.* Even now, acting so sweetly demure, her innocence attracted him like a flame. He remembered the fire of passion inside her. And how he was the only man who'd ever tasted it.

He felt himself tighten.

Stop! he ordered himself. He wouldn't think about her in bed. He wouldn't want her. He did have some control over his own body, damn it!

She clenched her fingers against his sleeve, her face pressed into his crisply tailored shirt.

"So I have no one." Her voice was small, almost a whisper. "No parents. No brothers or sisters. No one."

He looked down at her, tipping her chin upwards so he could see the tears sparkling in her beautiful violet-blue eyes. "You have me."

She swallowed, searching his face as if trying to read the emotion behind his expression. He schooled his features into concern and admiration and the closest attempt at love he could manage, never having actually felt it.

A sigh came from her lips as she exhaled. A soft smile traced her lips. "And our baby."

He gave a single grim nod. Their baby was the reason he had to make sure his control over Eve was absolute. The reason he had to make her believe he cared about her.

It was no different, he thought sardonically, than she'd once done to him. He would lull her into believing she could trust him. Make her willingly marry him.

Then—oh, then…

The instant their marriage was final, his life's goal would be to make her remember the truth. He would be with her when she finally remembered. He would see her face as it fell.

And he would crush her. The thought of revenge made his heart glad.

Not revenge, he told himself. *Justice.*

Leaning forward, he held her closer in the backseat of the Rolls-Royce.

"Eve." He cupped her face in his large hands. "I want you to marry me."

Marry him?

Yes, Eve thought in a daze, looking up into his handsome face. Feeling his strong, rough hands against the softness of her skin, the warmth of his touch seared her, tracing down her neck to her breasts and lower still.

How could any man be so masculine, so beautiful, so powerful all at once? Talos was everything her tattered, empty, frightened soul had desired. He would protect her. Love her. He would complete her life.

Yes, yes, yes.

But even as the words rose to her lips, something stopped her. Something she couldn't understand made her pull her face away from his touch.

"Marry you?" she whispered. She searched his dark eyes, her heartbeat quickening in her chest. "I don't even know you."

He blinked. She saw that he was surprised. Then his eyebrows lowered into a frown.

"You knew me well enough to conceive my child."

She swallowed. "But I can't remember you," she said. "It wouldn't be fair to take you as my husband. It wouldn't be right."

"I was raised without a father. I do not intend my child to endure that. I will give our baby a name. Do not deny me," he said urgently.

Deny him? How could any woman deny anything to a man like Talos Xenakis?

But it didn't feel right.

With a deep breath, she turned away, glancing out at the passing scenery. It had changed since they'd left the outskirts of London, become soft and green beyond the rain-splattered windows. Trees had started to turn orange and yellow, rich autumnal colors between the green.

"Eve."

She looked back at Talos. He was so darkly handsome and powerful, and at the moment his sensual mouth was pressed into a hard line. He was clearly determined to have his way.

But something inside her made her resist him.

"Thank you for asking me to marry you," she said awkwardly. "It's very warm and loving. But my baby won't be born for months—"

"*Our* baby," he corrected her.

"And I can't be your wife when I can't even remember you."

"We'll see," he said softly. Silence fell on their drive as she watched the passing scenery. Finally, the car turned off the road to a smaller lane. She saw a redbrick Georgian mansion at the base of tree-covered hills, reflected in a wide gray lake.

"Is that my stepfather's house?" she breathed in shock.

"Yes."

The car drove up the long lane through the park and woodlands then stopped in front of the entrance. As Talos opened the door and helped her from the car, Eve looked up with an intake of breath. She craned her head back to get a good look at the mansion, with its striking Victorian Gothic parapets stabbing upward into the steel-gray sky.

Holding her hand over her eyes to block out the noon sunlight that had finally penetrated the clouds, she looked back at him. "I lived here as a teenager?"

"And now it is yours, along with a vast fortune."

She looked at him sharply. "How do you know?"

"You knew it yourself yesterday, when you attended the reading of the will."

"But how do *you* know?" she persisted.

He shrugged. "I'll make sure you get a copy of the will. Come." Taking her hand, he escorted her past the grand sweep of the front door. Inside the foyer, five servants waited to greet her, headed by the housekeeper.

"Oh, Miss Craig," the plump woman sniffed into her apron. "Your stepfather loved you so much. He would be so glad to see you've finally come home!"

Home? But it wasn't her home. Apparently, she'd barely set foot in this place for years!

But looking at the elderly housekeeper's sad face, Eve felt a sympathetic pang. She put an arm around her.

"He was a good man, wasn't he?" she said softly.

"Yes, that he was, miss. The best. And he loved you as his own natural-born child. Even though you weren't, and American to boot," she added, wiping her eyes. "He'd be so happy you've finally come back after so long."

Eve paused delicately. "Has it been so…?"

"Six, no, seven years. Mr. Craig always invited you back for Christmas, but…"

Her voice trailed off as she wiped tears with her apron.

"But I never came, did I?" Eve said.

The older woman shook her head wistfully.

Eve swallowed. Apparently she'd taken her stepfather's money and let him pay her bills as she shopped and partied her way around the world, but hadn't even had the grace to return for an occasional visit!

And now he was dead.

"I'm sorry," she whispered over the lump in her throat.

"Let me take you to your room. You'll find it's just as you left it last."

Shortly afterwards, the quietly sobbing housekeeper left them in Eve's old bedroom. In the darkness, with Talos behind her in the only light of the double doorway, Eve yanked back the black curtains, filling the room with gray light.

Turning back to get a good look at her room, she choked back a gasp of dismay. Everything was red and black, down to the king-sized black lacquer bed. Dramatic. Modern. Sexy.

Garish.

Talos leaned against the door frame as Eve looked through the room, desperate for something, anything that would tell her what she needed to know. She opened closet doors, running her hands idly over the new clothes that hung there. The clothes were like the room, sexy and dramatic. Powerful clothes for a woman who desired attention and knew how to wield it.

Eve shivered.

She pulled open the shelves, touching each item lightly with her hands. Black stiletto heels. A Gucci handbag. A Louis Vuitton suitcase. Finding her passport, she thumbed through it, searching for answers that weren't there. Zanzibar? Mumbai? Cape Town?

"You weren't kidding," she said slowly. "I do travel constantly. Especially for the last three months."

When he didn't reply, she turned back to face him. His face seemed carefully expressionless.

"Yes," was all he said. "I know."

She tossed the passport into her suitcase with the sexy clothes and shoes that all seemed foreign, as if they belonged to someone else. Leaning against the modern black four-poster bed, she looked around her with a heavy sigh. "There's nothing here."

"I told you."

Desolately, she went to the bookshelf. It held only faded fashion magazines, years out of date, and a few slender volumes on etiquette and charm. She picked up the book on top, a splashy pop-culture book and read the title out loud in dismay. *"How to Get Your Man?"*

"That's never been your problem." There was a distinct edge to his voice.

Her heart was breaking, and he was making jokes? She made a huffing sound and chucked the book in his general direction. He caught it midair.

"Look, Eve," he said evenly. "It all doesn't matter."

"It does matter—these things tell me who I am!" She jabbed her finger toward the closet. "I've just found out I was the kind of girl who only cared about her looks, who ignored a stepfather who loved me, and who never bothered to come home at Christmas." Tears rushed into her eyes. "And I let him die alone," she whispered. "How could I have been so cruel?"

Desolately, she picked up a dusty photo in a gilded frame. She saw the image of a man giving a cheeky wink, his arm around a beautiful dark-haired woman who was laughing with joy. Between them was a plump little girl with a big beaming smile and two missing front teeth.

She stared at the adults in the photo for a very long time, but no memories came back to her. They had to be her parents, but she couldn't remember them. Was she really that heartless? Did she truly have no soul?

"What did you find?"

"Nothing. It doesn't help." She threw the photograph across the room, where it bounced softly against her bed. She covered her face with her hands. "I can't remember them. I can't!"

Crossing the bedroom in three long strides, he took her by the shoulders. "I barely knew my parents, but it hasn't hurt me."

"It's not just the past," she whispered. "Why would you want to be with a person like me? Without substance, without heart?"

He didn't answer.

"And now it's all too late," she said over the lump in her throat. "I've lost my only family. I have no home."

"Your home is with me," he said in a low voice.

She looked up at him. The sunlight from the tall windows gently caressed his face, illuminating floating dust motes like tiny stars all around them in the red-and-black bedroom.

"Let me show you." He slowly stroked up her bare arms, his fingers light against her skin. "Marry me."

Electricity spread up her arms and down her body. She fought the urge to step closer to him, to press her body against his chest. Shaking her head, she breathed, "I can't."

"Why?" he growled.

"I don't want you to marry me out of pity!"

His hands suddenly moved around her, caressing her back through her dress, causing the black silk to slide deliciously over her body with his featherlight touch. "Pity is the last thing I feel for you."

She closed her eyes, leaning forward in spite of herself. Wanting more of his touch. Wanting to feel his warmth. His heat.

He pulled her more deeply into his arms. She felt the scent of him, the warmth of his body beneath his clothes.

"Come away with me," he whispered into her hair. "Come to Athens and be my bride."

She felt the hardness of his body against hers, the strength of his arms around her. He was so much taller and more powerful than she was. His hands ran softly along the edges of her hips, up the length of her back as her breasts crushed against his chest.

She swallowed, trembling. She licked her lips, moving her cheek against his shirt as she looked up at him. "I can't just run away," she sighed. No matter how she wished she could. "I need my memory back, Talos. I can't just float through the world not knowing who I am. I can't marry a virtual stranger, even if you're the father of my child—"

"So I'll take you to the place where we first met. To where we began." She felt his dark gaze fall upon her mouth as he said softly, "I'll show you the place where I first kissed you."

Her bones turned to liquid. She looked up at him, her heart pounding as she licked her lips involuntarily. "Where is that?"

His eyes were hot and dark. "In Venice."

"Venice," she repeated, and the word was a wistful sigh. She looked up at him with yearning, knowing she should refuse—knowing she should stay in London and see the specialist Dr. Bartlett had recommended.

But her refusal caught in her throat. Caught by her romantic dreams. *Caught by him.*

Talos reached down to stroke her tender bottom lip with his thumb, caressing her face with his powerful hands.

"Come to Venice," he said darkly. "I will show you everything." He cupped her face with both hands, holding her hard against his body as he looked down at her, commanding her with his gaze. "And then," he whispered, "you will marry me."

CHAPTER THREE

SUNLIGHT reflected off the water as they took the *motoscafo,* a private water taxi, from the Marco Polo Airport. The September weather was bright and warm as they crossed the lagoon, passing by the Piazza San Marco and the Bridge of Sighs on the way to their hotel.

Venice. Talos had never expected to return here again.

But sometimes, he thought grimly, a man had to change the playbook in the middle of the game. He would do whatever it took, be as romantic a fool as any man could be, in order to lure Eve into marriage before her memory returned.

He looked down at her in his arms as they crossed the water of the canal. Her eyes shone with wonder, her full pink lips were slightly parted as she gazed around the city with awe.

The same way every man who saw Eve looked at *her*.

Even right now in this water taxi. The young Italian driver kept glancing back in his mirror. Talos's bodyguard, Kefalas, was sitting in the seat behind them, and even he had looked at Eve a bit longer than strictly necessary.

Eve was freshly showered and had changed her clothes on his private flight from London. Her dark hair now fell in thick, glossy waves past her bare shoulders, brushing the nipples Talos could easily picture beneath that clinging red jersey dress. The dress showed off the top swell of her overflowing breasts beneath the spaghetti straps, and barely reached halfway down her creamy thighs. She'd put on lipstick, a red color that matched her dress. Her legs were slender and perfect, ending in sharp black stiletto heels.

He couldn't blame either of them for staring. Even though he wanted to kill them for it.

Strange, Talos thought, he'd never been jealous before of other men staring at Eve.

He'd always accepted it as his due. He'd taken it for granted that other men would always want what he, Talos, possessed.

But for the first time it caused his stomach to curl. Why? Because Eve was carrying his child? Because he intended to make her his wife?

His wife in name only, he reminded himself. To protect his unborn child. Not because he cared for Eve. He felt nothing for her but scorn. And, he was forced to admit, lust.

Giving the driver a hard stare until the young man blushed and returned his focus to the wheel, Talos pulled Eve closer against him on the seat. She leaned back against his chest, reaching her arms over his neck and smiling up at him.

"It's beautiful here." Her blue eyes were as warm as bluebells in a spring meadow. "Thank you for bringing me to Venice. Even though I'm sure it was very inconvenient…"

He smiled down at her. Taking her hand, he brought it to his lips.

"Nothing is inconvenient to me if it gives you pleasure," he said, and softly pressed his mouth against her skin.

He felt her shiver beneath his touch in the warm afternoon sun. The air was salty and fresh. In the distance, he could hear the calls of seagulls, hear the distant chiming of medieval church bells.

"You're so good to me," she whispered, visibly affected by the way he'd kissed her hand. The realization that she was almost like an innocent, easily swayed by sensual desire, lit a dark fire in his heart.

The femme fatale she'd once been had disappeared along with her memories, it seemed. Dressed in the red dress and lipstick she still looked just like the same arrogant, cruel, fascinating creature she'd been three months ago, but she'd changed completely. With her skittish reactions, her youthful naïveté, she was almost like a virgin.

Except she wasn't—she was pregnant with his baby. And while she'd certainly been a virgin before they'd met, she'd never been innocent!

Remembering how they'd conceived that baby, all of his limbs suddenly seemed to burn where he had contact with her. Looking down into her beautiful face, he saw the vulnerability in her blue eyes, saw her pupils dilate. He was reminded of those hot breathless weeks in Athens when her naked body had been beneath his own. When he'd thought that beneath her achingly beautiful, shallow surface something existed that might be truly rare—truly worth possessing.

And he'd kept right on thinking that up until the day he'd seen her having breakfast with his rival, coldly giving him evidence to destroy Talos's company.

Remember that moment, he told himself harshly. *Remember how she betrayed you—and why.*

But as Eve looked up at him dreamily beneath the elegant, decrepit palazzos of Venice, with the sunlight shining off the canals, all he could suddenly think was that he wanted to kiss her. Now. Hard. To brand her permanently as his, to punish those cherry-red lips until she gasped and cried out in his arms.

His hands tightened around her shoulders, his fingers gripping into her slight frame as he remembered their days and nights in June. He'd been addicted to bedding her. He'd been lost in a woman, in a way he'd never experienced before or since.

He considered himself ruthless. He considered himself strong. But she'd bested him and he'd never seen it coming.

Now, he hated her with all his heart.

But he still wanted her. Wanted her with a consuming desire that could destroy him, if he ever let down his guard.

He would never give in to her temptation. Even if his weeks of bedding her had been the most erotically charged experience of his life, he would never take her again. If he ever even kissed her, he might be lighting a flame that he could not control.

He watched her nervously lick her lips—those full, cherry-red lips that had once made him shudder and scream with desire so intense he'd literally thought it might kill him.

He could tell she was bewildered by the electric connection between them. She didn't understand it. Unlike the Eve he'd known, who'd kept her feelings so carefully hidden, this girl didn't guard her expression. Her thoughts were clearly bare on her angelically beautiful face.

Good, he told himself harshly. The perfect weapon to use against her. He would convince her to marry him. He would romance her. Woo her. Court her. *Lure her.* He would take her as his wife—today. By any means necessary.

Except one.

He would not take her to his bed. *He would not.*

Eve turned her face up toward the bright Italian sun from the windows of the boat, leaning back against Talos's strong, powerful body as the *motoscafo* bounced across the waves. The leather seat hummed beneath her thighs from the vibrations of the engine.

She took a deep breath of the sharp, salty air. Her skin felt warm. Her body felt hot all over as she leaned against Talos's hard chest. Even through his black shirt she could feel the heat off his skin.

Then he smiled down at her. His smile did all kinds of strange things to her, making her heart pound. Her days of darkness and emptiness in rainy London now seemed like a lonely dream. She was in Italy with Talos.

And their baby. She placed her hand on her still-flat belly.

The water taxi slowed, pulled near the dock of a fifteenth-century palazzo. She stared at the high pointed windows that embellished the crumbling red stucco facade with awe at its exotic Gothic beauty. "Is that where we're going?"

His black eyes gleamed as he looked down at her. "Our hotel."

Oh. Their hotel.

She swallowed as she climbed from the taxi to the dock, picturing what it would be like to share a room with this man. To share space. *To share a bed.*

Just thinking of it, she stumbled on the dock.

"Careful," Talos said gruffly, grabbing her arm to steady her. "You don't have your sea legs yet."

All the colors of Venice, the twisting, sparkling water, the bright blue sky and tall, red campanile tower of the nearby piazza, seemed to fade into the background with a swirl of color behind him.

"You're right," she said over the lump in her throat. "I don't."

They stood on the dock as his bodyguard-assistant, Kefalas, paid the young Italian taxi driver and organized the luggage. But all Eve could see was Talos.

He was so handsome and tall and strong, she thought. She felt his arms tighten around her, and she suddenly wondered if he was going to kiss her. The thought scared her. She jerked away from him nervously. "We will, um, get separate rooms, won't we?"

She heard a low, sensual laugh escape him as he shook his head.

She licked her lips. "But—"

"I don't intend to let you out of my sight." He came forward toward her on the dock, and it took every ounce of her courage not to back away. He loosely brushed a tendril back from the blowing salty breeze. Kissing her temple, he whispered, "Or out of my arms."

Enfolding her hand in his own, he drew her toward the palatial hotel, where they were whisked inside by the waiting staff.

As Eve walked through the exquisite lobby, past soaring gilded arches and the sweeping staircase, she became slowly aware of men's heads whipping around to stare at her, almost like spectators following a tennis match.

It would have been funny, if she hadn't felt like the yellow ball.

Why were they staring at her?

What was wrong with her?

The doorman gaped at her, then jumped to open the door.

The male clerk did a double take from the elaborate desk before he looked away, clearing his throat.

The group of Italian businessmen crossing the lobby weren't so discreet. Three young men in pinstriped suits stopped in place on the marble floor, staring at her with open jaws. One man jabbed another in the ribs with a grin. Speaking rapidly in Italian, he started to come toward her. His friend stopped him by grabbing his wrist, gesturing toward Talos with palpable fear. Apparently too cowed by Talos to approach her, all three men continued to stare at her, murmuring soft words of appreciation.

Eve felt vulnerable.

Exposed.

Her cheeks went hot beneath all the scrutiny.

She was grateful when Talos took her hand and led her toward the elevator. She could feel all the men in the lobby stare after her, hear their mournful sighs meld with the click of her stiletto heels on the marble floor. They were probably staring at her backside right now.

Her neck broke out into a cold sweat.

Why were they staring at her?

Then in a flash, she knew.

The dress.

The tiny red dress that she'd taken from her bedroom closet in Buckinghamshire. Compared to the rest of the wardrobe, she'd thought it the simplest, easiest choice, comfortable and casual. It had seemed like a nice, though somewhat small, sundress in stretchy fabric. And since she apparently owned no comfortable shoes whatsoever, she'd chosen the black stiletto sandals, which at least wouldn't squeeze her toes. After her shower, she'd brushed out her dark hair and tentatively put on the lipstick in her handbag.

She'd hoped she would get used to her own clothes, feel confident in them.

Boy, had she been wrong.

Though the knit fabric was indeed soft

and stretchy, it was no match for her pregnant breasts, which spilled out quite distressingly over the top. The stiletto heels made her legs very long but also caused her hips to thrust forward and sway with every commanding step.

Comfortable? Casual?

Her clothes cried out for male attention, and no matter where they went, men's eyes centered on her. No matter their nationality, no matter their age or profession, men couldn't stop staring!

She didn't just look trashy, she realized with a horrified intake of breath. She looked like a tart who got paid by the hour!

When the penthouse door finally closed, and the teenaged bellhop left them with one last surreptitious, appreciative glance at Eve's breasts, she let out a huge sigh of relief. Thank heaven, she was finally alone with Talos!

Then she realized…

She was alone with Talos.

Nervously, she glanced around the lavish suite. Beneath the frescoed ceiling, a crystal chandelier sparkled over the old paintings, marble fireplace and gilded furniture. Thick, tasseled curtains parted at the wide windows to reveal a veranda that overlooked the canal. Multiple rooms graced the suite, including a living area and elegant bathroom.

But there was only one bed.

The enormous four-poster stood at the center of the suite. Eve couldn't take her eyes off it.

"Shall we go to dinner?" Talos purred from behind her.

Red-faced, she whirled around to face him, praying he wasn't able to read minds.

"Dinner? Out?" Thinking of all those leering masculine eyes, she shook her head desperately. "I don't really feel like going out tonight."

"Perfect," he said with a sensual curve of his lips. "So we'll stay in."

He came another step toward her, larger and more powerful than any man had a right to be. This royal suite was the size of a house, and yet he somehow filled every inch of the space, filled it to a breaking point. And if he did that to a four-thousand-square-foot suite...

She could only imagine what he'd do to a woman.

No! she wouldn't think about that. Her

cheeks flushed with heat. Nervously, she turned toward the window, feeling for all the world like a teenage virgin. She looked out the window across the sparkling water toward the Venetian island on the other side of the lagoon. She could see hotels, palazzos, ferries. She could see parked black gondolas rise and fall in the water in the wake of each passing speedboat bringing tourists to St. Mark's Square.

She felt him touch her shoulder.

"Is this the same hotel we stayed at before?" she stammered. "When we first met?"

"I stayed here alone," he said, looking down at her. "You refused to come up to my suite."

She whirled around to face him. "I did?"

"I tried to change your mind." Reaching down, he caressed her cheek. She took a deep breath at the gentleness of his touch, of his woodsy masculine scent that caused such shivers down her body. He said softly, "You resisted me."

"I did?" she blurted out. "How?" Then she blushed.

He gave a low laugh. His featherlight fingertips moved down her cheek toward her lips. He touched her so softly that she had to strain to feel him, almost as if he weren't quite touching her—forcing her to rise to meet him, whether she willed it or no. His fingers ran softly above the length of her tender bottom lip.

He leaned forward to whisper in her ear.

"You made me chase you. Harder and longer than I've ever chased any woman. No woman has ever been—will ever be—your equal."

As he pulled away from her, Eve's heart was pounding, each rise and fall of her breath shallow and quick.

His dark eyes gleamed down at her as if he knew exactly the tumult he'd created inside her. He was only maybe ten years older than her, and yet he somehow made her feel as though he had twice her strength and about a thousand times her experience!

"So. Shall we go out?" He glanced back at the bed. "Or stay in?"

Stay in this penthouse suite, which for all of its square footage suddenly felt tiny? Spend the evening alone with this powerful man, who made her feel such strange things, knocking her world off-kilter?

"I changed my mind. Let's go out!" she blurted, then blushed at her own nervousness. She felt like a shy young girl, a million miles out of her league.

"So you're hungry after all." At his low laugh, she knew she'd betrayed herself again, but she couldn't help it. Casually, he took her white trenchcoat from the closet, slinging it over one arm. He placed his other hand possessively against the small of her back, and his light touch made her sizzle all over.

Eve almost sighed with the relief of leaving the gorgeous suite—with its enormous bed— safely behind them.

As she followed him out of the hotel into the dusky streets of Venice, she didn't know it would be a classic case of out of the frying pan, into the fire.

CHAPTER FOUR

THE sun was starting to set in earnest, giving the twilight a pink-and-orange glow with a rapidly chilling autumn bite in the air. As a light fog blew in from the lagoon, Talos reached for Eve's hand.

His hand wrapped around her smaller one, their naked palms pressing together, and she gave an involuntary shiver that had nothing to do with the cooling night.

He paused on the walkway between the piazzetta and the canal. "Cold?"

She nodded, because how could she tell him the truth? How could she tell him that his every touch exhilarated and frightened her in equal measure?

"That won't do." Behind his head, she could see the Byzantine white domes, arches and sharp spires of St. Mark's Basilica. Sunset caressed his handsome face in warm reddish-pink light. "Here."

He took the trenchcoat he'd carried on his arm and wrapped it around her. He was so handsome, she thought in a daze as she tied the belt of her coat. So starkly powerful, wearing a black wool coat over a black tailored shirt and black pants. For a moment, she just looked at him, catching her breath.

Then a group of young men walked past them and she heard a low whistle. She looked down and blushed, realizing her slim-fitting white trenchcoat covered her red dress completely. With her legs and collarbone bare, she must look as if she were naked beneath it!

She bit her lip. "Maybe we should take a taxi?"

"The restaurant is close," he said tersely. "Just on the other side of the square." He took her arm, placing it over his own. His eyes were dark as he looked down at her. "Come."

It was incredibly romantic, watching the sun lower over the Grand Canal. Romantic, but not comfortable. Her black stiletto heels twisted her ankles as she walked, but that wasn't the worst thing. She was continually aware of men staring at her as they passed by the walkway. And Talos was aware of it, too. She could tell by the way he held her arm tightly, glowering at any other man who came too close or stared too long. He was like a lion ready to fight, to kill, to protect his female.

Eve felt vulnerable. Like a gazelle about to get ripped to shreds for some lion's dinner. What difference did it make which lion?

She looked up at Talos beside her. Something about him scared her in a way she didn't understand. It was because she couldn't remember him, she told herself. If she did, surely she wouldn't be afraid…?

Behind them, she saw a shadowy figure following at a discreet distance. Nervously, she licked her lips, tasting lipstick flavored like wax and roses. "There's someone following us."

Talos glanced back, then relaxed. "Kefalas."

"Your bodyguard?"

"He'll only come if needed."

"But—"

"It's necessary." He looked down at her. The slant of the setting sun cast his brutally

handsome features in a roseate glow as he
added roughly, "Just to protect you from all
your Italian admirers, it seems."

"I don't like the attention," she whispered.
"I don't want them to stare at me."

She could tell by the twist to his lips that
he didn't completely believe her. Her cheeks
burned pink. She wished she were covered
from head to toe in a padded snowsuit.

Her clothes had to change, she thought.

Talos escorted her into a small hotel overlooking the Grand Canal, to the restaurant in
the back which had a lovely wide terrace with
a view of the water. The restaurant was
packed, but somehow they were immediately
taken to the best table.

Across the simple candlelit table, they
shared an amazing meal of seafood risotto
and tagliolini with scampi. The food was a
sensual experience. As she finished her
risotto, licking her fork with satisfaction, she
felt his gaze upon her. And even as the cool
night breeze drifted across her bare shoulders
and legs, she shivered with sudden heat.

Unable to bear the intensity of his gaze, she
looked away. Across the black shadows of

gondolas in the water, she saw a beautiful white domed church lit up in the night.

"That's Santa Maria della Salute," he said quietly. "You loved it last time, too."

"Last time?"

"Don't you remember this restaurant?"

"Should I?"

His dark eyes flickered at her in the candlelight. "We came here on our first date."

The waiter brought the dessert of tiramisu, but as she took her first bite of the sweet cake, she could hardly taste it. With a deep breath, she set down her fork. And met his eyes.

He reached for her hand over the table.

"I am glad I found you," he said in a low voice that made her tremble from within. "Glad you're here now."

He was still being so kind and loving to her. She could hardly understand it. She covered her face with one hand.

"You must hate me," she said in a low voice.

His fingers seemed to tighten by reflex over her other wrist. "Why do you say that?"

Tears filled her eyes as she looked up at him. "Because I can't remember you! You are my lover, the father of my child, and you're being so kind to me. You're trying so hard to help me remember. But it's useless, all useless, because my brain—won't—*work!*"

Her voice choked as tears spilled down her cheeks. Aware she was making a scene, desperate to escape all the eyes on her—now those of the women, too, as well as the men—Eve pulled away from him. Throwing her linen napkin on the table, she ran outside.

Talos caught up with her a few moments later, her coat in his arms.

"It's all right," he murmured. He kissed her temple and she felt his hands in her long, loose hair. "It's all right."

"It's not all right," she choked out, gulping back tears. She looked up at him. "How can I be with you and not remember?"

"You need to calm down," he said in a low voice. "This can't be good for the baby— being pushed all over Venice."

"You haven't pushed me. You've been gentle and wonderful." She wiped the tears away angrily. "It's my fault. All mine. Dr. Bartlett said there's no physical reason that I shouldn't remember. So what is it? What's wrong with me?"

He clenched his jaw. "I don't know."

"Maybe I should go back to London. See that specialist—"

"No." His dark gaze caught hers, sensual and intense. He cupped her face with his hands. "You don't need any doctors. You just need time. Time and care. And me. I remember enough for both of us. Marry me, Eve. Make me happy."

Her face felt warm where he touched her. His eyes fell to her mouth, and her lips tingled beneath his gaze as if he'd touched her with his hands. And immediately, her whole body felt sparked, consumed by raging fire, like dry tinder sparked by lightning.

Behind him, she saw the famous Piazza San Marco, toward the tall red campanile and the famous domed white basilica that was as exotic as anything in Cairo or Istanbul. The hour was late, the night was magic, the tourists had melted away into the mists, leaving the two of them alone, drenched in moonlight beside the water.

He was going to kiss her.

She wanted him to kiss her. Ached for it.

As he slowly lowered his head to hers,

her whole body vibrated, leaning forward, yearning…

But as she closed her eyes and leaned up for his kiss, she suddenly found herself standing five feet away from him.

She could see the rapid, hoarse rise and fall of his breath as he stared at her in the moonlight with eyes so dark they seemed black.

"What is it, Eve?" he said in a low voice. "Why did you jump away?"

"I don't know," she whispered helplessly over the lump in her throat. "I want to kiss you, but for some reason, I'm…afraid."

He gave a sudden low laugh, a sensual, knowing sound that caused a rumble to echo off the waves of the water. "You're right to be afraid."

"What do you mean?" she asked, unable to look away.

Reaching for her hand, he kissed her palm. "This fire could consume us both." Slowly, he kissed each knuckle of her hand, causing zings of pleasure to curl up and down her body. "Once I start kissing you, I might never stop."

A shudder of pleasure went through her at those words. Pleasure…desire…fear.

But his face was so strangely dark in the moonlight.

She couldn't blame his mood, she told herself. Not when she'd been so weepy a moment before!

"Come," he said in a low voice. "It's late. Time for bed."

For…bed?

Her knees shook beneath her as he led her back to the hotel. She barely noticed the beautiful sights of Venice, the lights on the gondolas or the islands across the water. All she could see in her mind's eye was the penthouse suite waiting for them.

The *bed* waiting for them.

Biting her lip, she glanced at him sideways through her lashes. He was so breathtakingly handsome and strong. But beyond just his incredible sexiness, he was a good man. He'd been nothing but loving and patient. He hadn't been angry or hurt about the fact she couldn't remember him. No, his only focus had been on making her comfortable. On helping her.

No, that wasn't true. He wanted something else.

He wanted to marry her.

The father of her child, a handsome, powerful Greek tycoon, wanted to marry her. So why couldn't she accept? Why couldn't she at least let him kiss her? Why wouldn't her body let her?

You're right to be afraid.

She heard more low whistles and muttered appreciation in Italian as they passed a new group of young men. Clenching his hands, Talos started to turn toward them. His whole body seemed abruptly tight and angry, almost enraged. He meant to fight them all, she realized. He was suddenly bruising for a fight.

Frightened, she stopped him with a gentle touch on his wrist. "Can I have my coat back?" she implored. "I'm so cold."

He instantly turned back to face her. "Of course, *khriso mou.*" Looking down at her, he tenderly wrapped the coat around her. For a moment, she was lost in his dark gaze. He took her hand in his own. "I'll get you back to the hotel."

Eve exhaled, relieved she'd distracted him before he could start a fight with those young Italians. From the look on Talos's face, she'd been afraid. *For them.* He'd been taut with fury that seemed far beyond what their fairly innocent provocation had deserved.

But she wouldn't allow it to happen again. As they walked past the doorman and into the lobby, Eve vowed she would change her wardrobe completely.

Once inside their penthouse suite, Talos immediately released her hand. When she came out of the bathroom ten minutes later, after brushing her teeth, he didn't even glance up from the sleek desk near the window where he was working on his laptop. Through the window behind him, she could see the twinkling lights of ferries crossing from the Adriatic Sea.

"Thank you for loaning me your pajama top," she said awkwardly. She gave a laugh that sounded nervous and goofy, even to her own ears. "I must have lost mine. There was nothing in my suitcase."

"You always slept in the nude."

She swallowed, staring at his profile, very aware of the bed behind her. "Well, um…"

"You take the bed." Standing up, he closed his laptop and finally looked at her. His dark gaze, which had been so hot when he'd nearly kissed her near St. Mark's Square, had suddenly cooled. "I'll work in the office so I don't disturb you. I'll sleep on the couch when I'm tired."

After the amount of time she'd spent trying to steady her nerves and steel herself to share a hotel room, she'd never expected this—for him to treat her as if she were a distant guest. She glanced from his tall body and wide shoulders to the small, slender couch. "You won't be able to fit on that!"

"I'll manage." He turned away. "You and the baby need rest." Rising from the desk, he left the room. He paused at the door. "Good night."

He turned off her light. Since she had no other choice, she climbed into bed and pulled the covers up to her neck. Bereft of his warmth. Miserable. Alone.

She sighed as she turned her head back and forth on the thick, luxurious pillow, trying to get comfortable, trying to make herself sleep with anxious thoughts racing circles in her mind.

Why hadn't she let him kiss her?

She'd yearned to know what it would feel like to have his mouth on hers. She sighed now just thinking about it. And yet she'd jumped away from him without thought. As if she'd placed her hand on a burning stove.

She heard the echo of his dark, haunted voice. *You are right to be afraid.*

Afraid? Eve flipped onto her other side with an impatient huff of breath. Afraid of what? Talos was a good man. Her lover. The father of her child. He'd been so loving, so romantic, so patient with her!

And he wanted to *marry* her.

She needed to do whatever it took to regain her memory, for Talos's sake. For their baby's sake. For her own.

Tomorrow, she promised herself firmly. Tomorrow, she would be brave. Tomorrow, she would let him kiss her.

When Talos woke up the next morning, Eve was gone.

He sat up on the couch with an intake of breath. Looking at the bright light from the windows, he knew he'd overslept; the clock over the mantel said eleven. Where was Eve? He looked at the king-sized bed.

It was empty. Empty and *made*.

She'd made the bed?

With a growl deep in his throat, he stood up, dropping his blankets and pillow haphazardly to the floor. Then he saw the little note in her handwriting written on hotel stationary, neatly affixed to the top pillow.

Gone shopping. Back soon.

He exhaled. So she hadn't regained her memory and run away. He'd ordered Kefalas to keep an eye on her in any case. She wouldn't escape him again.

Eve was out shopping. A humorless smile traced his lips. Apparently she hadn't changed as much as he'd thought.

With a yawn, he raised his arms over his head, stretching his half-naked body. His chest was bare, his legs in pajamas. Every muscle ached, and it wasn't just because he'd managed to fit his six-foot-three frame into a couch that was at most five foot ten. It was from being so close to Eve.

Listening to her breathe.

Remembering the last time he'd slept in a room with her.

The last time she'd been in his bed.

He clawed back his hair. Spending the whole day with her yesterday, pretending to be her devoted lover, had been difficult. Spending the whole night in the same hotel room without trying to seduce her had nearly killed him.

He hated that he still wanted her.

She'd been perfect three months ago, her figure slender but curvaceous in all the right places, but now her newly pregnant breasts were so lush, while her waist was still so tiny, that she was the epitome of any man's dream.

Including his.

He'd purposely stayed in the next room until 3:00 a.m., answering e-mails and making long phone calls to Australia about the Sydney deal. He'd purposefully waited until he'd nearly passed out over his keyboard before he allowed himself to stumble back into the dark bedroom and fall on the couch. As the window's light changed to the grayness of dawn, he'd finally collapsed with exhaustion.

But even in sleep, he'd had endless dreams of making love to her. He'd woken up hard for her.

With a loud curse, Talos twisted his head to crack the vertebrae in his neck. He hurt all over.

Stomping into the bathroom, he turned on the shower then stared blankly at the rapidly steaming water.

He'd always known Eve was shallow and selfish. But he'd been intrigued by all her contradictions, his seductive virgin mistress, the gorgeous beauty who never asked him questions or revealed any of her feelings. Unlike any other woman, she'd taken pleasure in bed without emotion.

He'd been captivated by her. When she was naked beneath him in bed, when he brought her to a gasping climax, her blue eyes had shone up at his with sudden searing vulnerability. He'd thought there was something more inside her soul. Some mystery that only he could solve.

And he'd kept on believing that, right up till the day she'd sneaked from their bed, rifled through his private safe and stolen damaging financial information to give to Jake Skinner over a romantic breakfast.

Overnight, the Xenakis Group's stock had crashed nearly in half, causing him to lose nearly the whole company with margin calls. If Talos hadn't had the resources of his personal fortune to back him up, he would have lost his company. He would have lost everything.

Instead of buying distressed companies at pennies on the dollar, he would have been one of the poor fools forced to sell.

He cursed softly in Greek.

And in spite of all that, he'd nearly kissed her tonight. He'd wanted to take her against the wall of an alley in view of the Bridge of Sighs and possess her utterly. Over and over. Until he had his fill.

He was so tense with fighting his desire for her, that when those Italians had dared to whistle at Eve, he'd almost thrown himself at them. He'd suddenly relished the thought of the relief of pain, of punching them all bloody in an honest fight.

How simple a straightforward street fight had seemed, compared to trying to lure the woman he hated—the woman he wanted—into marriage!

Clenching his fists, Talos stepped into the shower. He leaned back as the hot water coursed over his naked body. He washed his hair, rubbed soap over his chest.

Would it be so bad to give in to temptation?

The insidious thought made his eyes fly open.

Would it be so bad to take what he wanted? To gorge himself until he was sick of her?

Like Scotch.

The first time he'd tasted an expensive single malt Scotch, he'd been only nineteen, newly arrived in New York. He'd done well for his American boss in Athens, but this was a new country—a new world. Waiting for half an hour in Dalton Hunter's office, he'd grown steadily more nervous. He'd finally poured himself a shot of the rich amber-colored liquor from a crystal decanter on a silver tray. He'd had one delicious taste before he'd looked up to see Dalton watching him from the door.

Wondering if he was about to get sacked on his first day, Talos lifted his chin and observed defiantly, "I thought you'd want me to learn how to hold my liquor. As an asset to the company."

"Quite so," Dalton said, sounding amused. Then his eyes narrowed. "So drink it all."

Talos had looked at the nearly full decanter in shock. "All?"

"Right now. Or get out."

So Talos had drunk the entire decanter, gulping down the smooth, smoky Scotch as if it were water. However, his bravado had been lessened when he'd spent the whole afternoon puking in the office bathroom, aware of the other employees laughing at him in the hallway. When he'd finally gone back to his boss, he'd been red-faced, sweaty, humiliated.

"Now you know not to steal from me," Dalton had said before he coldly turned away. "Get to work."

Talos still grimaced as he remembered that day. He'd never been able to touch Scotch again. Almost twenty years later, just the smell of it still made him sick.

And that was how he wished he could feel about Eve.

He wished he could get her out of his system once and for all. Until he never wanted her again. Until the thought of bedding her was as disgusting as a flawless Baccarat crystal decanter of imported single malt Scotch.

Turning off the water, he toweled himself dry. He pulled his clothes from the closet where someone in his staff had neatly put them away. He stepped into his boxers and black pants, then stared at himself in the half-fogged mirror. He took a deep breath.

No.

He wouldn't give in to lust.

He wouldn't be seduced by her again.

Fiercely, he pushed aside the thought of Eve in his bed, her skin glowing with rough lovemaking and her eyes full of desire.

He'd once planned to take her new fortune from her under threat of prosecuting her for theft and corporate espionage.

But now…

All he wanted was their child, safe and healthy in his arms. And Eve to disappear from their lives forever after the baby was born.

As he buttoned his sharply tailored white shirt, he glared at himself in the mirror. Every time he thought of the lustful fool he'd been a few months ago, neglecting his business, spending every hour in bed with her, making love to her day and night, it made him grind his teeth with rage.

He would never let it happen again.

He would never lower his guard. Never give up control again.

Talos had to convince her to marry him as soon as possible. Today, he thought, leaning in toward the mirror as he shaved his jaw. He couldn't risk her regaining her memory before he'd tied her down as his bride, giving his child a name. Then he would help her remember. And after the baby was born, he would blackmail Eve with the choice of her child or her money.

He had no doubt which she'd choose.

So today, he would act the part of a besotted lover. He would tempt her. Lure her. He would whisper sweet words. Poetry. Flowers. Jewelry. Whatever it took. His lip curled. How hard could it be?

He dropped the razor to the counter, wiping the last vestiges of shaving cream off his face with a towel.

He would not, repeat, would not—he glared at himself—take her to his bed.

Damn it, he wouldn't!

He heard a door slam and suddenly Eve was standing behind him. His jaw dropped as he looked at her in the mirror. She smiled back serenely.

"Good morning."

"Eve." He whirled around with a gasp. "What have you done?"

CHAPTER FIVE

EVE had been beaming at him, but now she felt suddenly shy. She put her hand to her hair, which yesterday had hung past her breasts but now barely touched her collarbone. "I had my hair cut."

"I can see that."

"So why did you ask?" she retorted pertly, squaring her shoulders. "Honestly!"

He ignored that, walking around her in a circle in the wide marble bathroom, looking her up and down.

She lifted her chin defiantly, daring him to criticize her.

The sleekly modern, rather than sexy, blunt-cut pageboy hairstyle wasn't her only change. Instead of the tight red dress and overflowing cleavage she'd had last night, she was now dressed in a cotton jersey cardigan and long knit skirt in pale rose. The simple garments were still pretty, she hoped, but natural—not to mention stretchy against her expanding pregnancy. And the pink flat sandals were certainly easier to wear than the stiletto heels.

She now felt comfortable in her own skin rather than like someone trying to gain attention through her clothing.

But he only frowned at her.

"I don't understand," he muttered, lifting his hand as if to touch her, then dropping it again. "Where did you buy this?"

"At a boutique in the Mercerie recommended by the concierge."

"Did you take Kefalas with you?"

"Yes," she sighed. "I didn't want to, but he insisted on it. He wouldn't even let me use the credit cards in my purse, but insisted I charge everything to your accounts."

"Good." He peered down at her. "You look different," he mumbled.

Different as in bad? She shuffled her feet, feeling awkward under his scrutiny.

"Why the makeover?" he asked, tilting his head.

She took a deep breath. How could she explain how horrifying it had been to have men constantly gawking at her? How to explain how wretched she'd felt when Talos had nearly started a brawl against five men just because of some strangers' low whistles and murmured appreciation of her charms that were too flagrantly on display? She licked her bare lips.

"Um," she managed, "the clothes in my suitcase just, er, didn't fit right."

He lifted a dark eyebrow. "That's not what you said when I bought them for you in Athens."

"You bought the clothes?" she blurted out. "Even the red dress?"

"Yes."

She swallowed. Now she'd sounded ungrateful. "They were all lovely. Really. But…"

"But?"

"But they're not comfortable. They, um, made people look at me."

He stared at her. "I thought you liked that."

"It was still a lovely gift," she stammered.

"And I'm so grateful. That you picked them out for me is terribly sweet."

"Lovely?" he repeated in a surly voice. *"Sweet?"*

"And I don't mean to be critical of your taste, but—"

"I didn't pick them out for you," he ground out. "I just paid for them. You chose."

She had? What had she been thinking? "Oh. Um. Don't worry, I'm sure the charity shops will sell them quickly," she said apologetically. "They're so glamorous—so well-made!"

He glanced at her empty suitcase with surprise. Glanced at the many bags that Kefalas had just left inside the doorway before discreetly disappearing.

"You gave away all your designer clothes?" he said incredulously. "The Gucci? The Versace?"

"Are they your favorite designers?" she said, chagrined to be so rude.

"No!" he nearly shouted. "They're yours!"

"Oh," she said. She bit her lip. "Well, those clothes are just a little too tight for me now. Not to mention too sexy." She brightened as a sudden explanation occurred to her.

"Maybe my tastes have changed because I'm about to be a mother," she said happily, relieved to have an explanation. "That's probably it, don't you think?"

He stared at her. He started to speak, then visibly bit back the words. Finally, he silently held out his arm. She took it in her own.

"You look beautiful," he said quietly.

She peeked up at him, hoping he really meant it. "Really?"

"Yes." He gave her a slow-rising smile. It lit up his face, making him so handsome that he took her breath away. Reaching down, he stroked her bare cheek. "I've never seen you look more radiant."

She exhaled. She hadn't realized until that moment that she'd been tense, wondering what his reaction would be. She'd cut her hair. She'd gotten rid of the low-cut, tight dress and the stiletto heels. Would he still approve of her? Would he still want her in his life?

His hot, smoldering glance told her that yes, he approved, and yes, he wanted her.

The *real* her. Without all the tarty trimmings.

"Now," he said as his smile sharpened, "let's go get what we came here for."

For the rest of the day, they explored the charms of Venice, from walking beneath the medieval overhangs of the Calle del Paradiso to sharing lunch on the wide outdoor terrace of the Hotel Cipriani.

The fog thickened throughout the afternoon as the capricious autumn weather turned melancholy. But Eve barely noticed that the Italian sunshine had disappeared. As they strolled along canals as gray as the lowering sky, she felt warm and contented. Talos smiled down at her, his dark eyes warming her with the heat of burning coal as they laughed and talked, walking down the tree-lined paths through the grassy Giardini.

He bought her a fiery orange rose from a stall in an outdoor market. When he told her in a low voice how beautiful she was to him, how much he wanted her to be his wife, she glowed from within. She barely heard the sad, plaintive cries of the gulls soaring through the heavy clouds overhead.

As the afternoon drew on, rain finally started to drizzle. The fair-weather tourists had scattered beneath the cold-blowing winds, but Eve had never felt more gloriously lit up inside.

In her new clothes, she got occasional second glances from men, but only from up close—not from across the street. She wasn't forced to endure the endless hot stares of strange men, while knowing that only the presence of powerful, darkly dangerous Talos kept the other males at bay.

Now, she felt safe.

She felt…free.

She never wanted the day to end. She glanced down at his hand in hers as they walked. He was so possessive, so attentive. So romantic and loving.

She felt his eyes on her constantly. Any time she turned her head, she caught his gaze. Even when he didn't touch her, she felt his presence like electricity. Like fire.

As the rain started to fall more heavily, he drew her back inside an elaborate Gothic doorway. Then, to her surprise, he turned around to knock on the door of the palazzo.

"What are we doing here?" she asked, confused.

"You'll see."

They were admitted by a housekeeper. She told them in heavily accented English that, sadly, his friends the marchese and marchesa were away on vacation. But when Talos, with his most charming smile, asked to see the ballroom, she could not resist.

Who could? Eve thought.

Once the housekeeper left them alone in the enormous gilded ballroom, beneath the medieval fifteenth-century timbers and decorated stucco rosework, Eve could not believe the ballroom's size or beauty. To get a better view, she walked halfway up the sweeping stairs.

"And that is where I first saw you," Talos said in a low voice behind her.

She whirled around. "Here?"

"At the charity ball the first weekend in June."

The sun shone weakly through the tall windows of the palazzo, leaving a tracery of the Gothic rose pattern of the facade on the marble floor. She could almost imagine long-ago pirates coming to plunder the wealth of La Serenissima.

"Before that day," he said, staring at the sunlight through the multicolored glass of the windows, "I'd scoffed at the rumors about you. No woman could be that beautiful, I said. No woman could be that mesmerizing." Slowly, he turned to look at her. His dark eyes sizzled through her as he said in a low voice, "Then we met."

Talos looked just like the dark corsair she'd imagined, the Barbary pirate who'd come to plunder the medieval city—to take what he wanted and burn the rest.

She blinked. How had she come up with such a brutal, cruel image? Where had that come from?

"I saw you coming down those stairs in a long red dress," he said softly. "You were on the arm of my greatest business rival, but I knew at once that I would take you from him." Slowly, he walked up the stairs toward her. "I would have taken you from the devil himself."

As he came up the stairs toward her, she was unable to move. *Unable to breathe.*

"You made me pursue you across Venice for a week before you finally surrendered and agreed to accompany me to Athens. Where I finally discovered to my surprise that you were a virgin." He fixed his dark eyes on her and a flash of heat coursed through her body. "For the first time in my life, I found myself wanting a woman *more* after I had bedded her, instead of less."

He bent his head toward her. She couldn't move, couldn't breathe.

"The more I had of you," he whispered, "the more I wanted."

But as he lowered his head to kiss her, he suddenly stopped, then stiffened. Without touching her, he wrenched away, his eyes cold. "Come. We're done here."

After thanking the housekeeper, he led her from the palazzo. Outside, as the storm clouds brewed above them, she could feel a storm building between them as well, a tension that had nothing to do with tenderness.

He led her across an elaborate covered bridge that crossed the Grand Canal. It was momentarily empty of tourists, and as the cold, wet wind howled around them, he finally turned to face her.

His eyes were dark and hot.

A little thrill of jumbled fear and desire went through her as he took her in his arms. She felt his fingers brush her skin, felt his muscular body hard against hers. The tension increased inside her, tightening into a coil low in her belly.

"This," he said hoarsely, "is where I first kissed you."

He leaned forward, stroking the back of her head. Brushing stray tendrils from her cheek, he cupped her face with his hands. Staring up at his handsome face, she was aware of tiny details. The dark scruff on his chin, though he had shaved just hours before. She'd thought his eyes were black, but now she saw they were a deep brown, with slivers of honey-gold.

"And," he said in a low voice, lowering his head toward her, "this is where I'm going to kiss you now."

She trembled all over, her heart pounding like a frantic hummingbird's wing. She wanted him to kiss her—but at the same time something pushed her to flee!

But she couldn't. This time, he held her fast. He wouldn't let her back away.

It was as if she'd never been kissed before. His lips were gentle at first on her mouth. Then he spread her lips wide. He teased her with his tongue, licking her lips, entwining her tongue with his.

Desire and need swept through her like a fire. And she forgot about running away. She couldn't resist. *She didn't want to.*

His kiss hardened, deepened. Instead of tempting and luring, he suddenly demanded and took. His body pressed against hers so tightly she was no longer sure where he ended and she began.

The kiss was like nothing she'd felt before.

Just like a kiss should be.

She was dazed, lost in him. As he pulled away, a small whimper of protest escaped her. He looked down at her. There was a fire in his dark eyes.

"Now, *glyka mou*," he whispered. "You belong to me."

Above their heads, she could hear the caw of seagulls soaring high above, hear the ringing of the distant church bells. She could hear the lap of the water beneath them, the sound of a speedboat, hear the cries of vendors from the nearby Rialto market.

You belong to me. She closed her eyes as the echo of those words went through her. He'd spoken those words to her before. He'd kissed her here before.

You belong to me.

That hot, humid summer night, the moon had been full, washing both of them in veils of silver. She remembered the press of his hands against her bare shoulders, over her dress. She remembered desperately wanting him to kiss her. Remembered a sense of relief and triumph as he took her in a hard, savage kiss. Remembering sinking into his arms, so tight, so tight, at last...

Eve's eyes flew open as she drew back from him with an intake of breath. "I remembered something!"

Talos's eyes widened. Then his jaw tightened.

"What exactly did you remember?" he said, his voice low and strained, but in her excitement, she didn't pause to wonder why. She gave him a joyful smile as tears rose to her eyes.

"Our first kiss. It was here on this bridge, just like you said! Oh, Talos, I'm getting my memory back. It's coming back! Everything is going to be all right!"

She threw her arms around him, holding him tightly, overwhelmed by gratitude and relief. She pressed her face to his chest, squeezing her eyes shut to hold back the tears.

Her mind might not remember much about him, but her body instinctively did. She'd been so afraid, but now…

But now…

As she held him, her heart quickened, galloping faster and faster. The mood between them suddenly changed, electrified. A moment before, she'd just been joyful to have a memory to cling to, some sense of who she was and her past. But as he held her body close, as she breathed in the scent of his skin and pressed her cheek against his soft black shirt, she suddenly felt quite different.

Her cheeks grew hot as she looked up into his eyes.

"Eve, my beautiful Eve," he whispered, touching her face. "Marry me. Be my wife."

Yes, she opened her mouth to say.

But she forced herself to shake her head. "You deserve so much more," she said softly. "You deserve a wife who can remember everything about loving you."

His lips curled with a faint hint of mockery. "Don't worry. I'll get what I deserve." He paused, then his eyes glowed down at her. "After you are my wife, I will devote myself night and day to helping you remember your past. I swear it."

She swallowed, picturing how wonderful it would be to be his wife. How right it would be, to be married as they awaited the birth of their child. Perhaps then her body wouldn't be so afraid for him to kiss her.

Perhaps her sense of honor would accept far more than a kiss.

"It would be selfish of me to accept," she gasped, clinging to her decision by her fingernails.

He traced her tender, bruised lower lip with his fingertip. "It would be selfish of you to refuse. Marry me. For the baby's sake." He paused. "For mine."

She shuddered as his stroke against her lip sent sparks down her body, making her nipples tighten, causing her to shiver all over.

He thought she was being selfish when she was only refusing him for his own sake?

She exhaled. She couldn't fight it anymore. Not when all she wanted to do was be loved and protected and make sure her baby was, too.

"Marry me," he murmured between kisses to her eyelids, her forehead, her throat. She could hardly think straight. He held her so gently, so tenderly. With such love. "Marry me now."

Her eyes were blurry with tears as she stared up at his darkly handsome face. There was a halo of light behind his head, and in the distance she could see birds flying up through the darkly shifting gray sky.

Then he lowered his lips to hers.

Her last thought before he kissed her was that she couldn't remember loving him, but perhaps she didn't need to remember.

Perhaps…she could just fall in love with him all over again.

CHAPTER SIX

KISSING Eve was like falling into hell.

It was fire. Sheer fire running through him. Talos placed his hand on the back of her head, his fingers twining in her beautiful hair, as he deepened the kiss.

For months, he'd hated her. *Hungered for her.*

Was that why finally kissing her now overwhelmed his senses more than ever before?

It wasn't just desire that had changed the kiss, he realized. It was Eve. The kiss was different because *she* was different.

Wrenching away, he looked down at her. Her eyes remained closed. A blissful smile traced her full, bare lips. In her new clothes and hairstyle, she appeared sweet, natural and true.

The Eve he remembered had been none of those things.

Her eyes were still closed as she leaned forward, licking her lips with a tiny dart of her pink tongue. He nearly groaned. He wanted to take her to bed. Now. He'd already started to pick her up to take her back to the hotel when he caught himself.

No!

He took a deep breath. He couldn't forget who he was really dealing with. The kind, innocent girl in front of him was an illusion. The real Eve Craig was a shallow vixen, a selfish liar. She'd given him her virginity just so she could betray him for another man. He couldn't let her win.

This time, the victory would be his.

"Marry me," he demanded, barely holding himself back from kissing her again. "Marry me now."

"All right," she whispered. "All right."

He exhaled in a rush. Pulling away, he looked down at her fiercely. "Today."

"I'll marry you today," she murmured, looking up at him with a happy, almost tearful smile.

"Talos? Getting married?" a man said behind them. "I can't believe I just heard that!"

Talos whirled around in consternation to see an old friend grinning at him. The man split his time between New York and Tuscany—what the hell was he doing in Venice?

"Roark," he said faintly. "What are you doing here?"

"I never thought I'd see this day," Roark Navarre replied with a snicker. "You always said you'd never get married. You gave me a hell of a time when I married Lia. How the mighty have fallen!" Laughing, he took a step forward. "I can't wait to meet the woman who—"

Then Eve shyly turned to face him, and the grin dropped from Roark's face.

He stopped, his eyes widening.

Eve snuggled back in Talos's arms. A pink blush suffused her cheeks as she looked at Roark with quiet happiness.

His old friend gave Talos a sharply questioning glance. "Is this some kind of joke?"

Eve blinked, furrowing her brow. She glanced between the two men. "What do you mean? A joke?"

"He just can't believe a woman like you would settle for a man like me," Talos told her lightly, then over Eve's head, he stared hard at Roark. "Isn't that right?"

His friend got the message. "Yes. Exactly right."

"I wouldn't say I'm settling exactly," Eve teased him, then looked back at Roark. "Have we met?"

Roark frowned, blinking as if he were in some kind of weird upside-down world. "Several times. At parties, mostly. You were once on a charity committee with my wife."

"Oh." Eve held out her hand with a friendly, apologetic smile. "I'm so sorry. I've had some memory problems lately. What's your name?"

"Roark Navarre. My wife is Lia."

"Lovely to meet you. Is she here?"

"No. She's at home with our kids in Tuscany." Roark shook her hand, then shot Talos a questioning look. "I came to Venice to buy her a gift. Today's our third wedding anniversary."

"How romantic!"

Roark cleared his throat. "Not as romantic as the two of you, it seems. You're really getting married today?"

"Yes," she said shyly, glancing back at Talos. She radiated contentment and quiet joy.

Roark had reason to look shocked, Talos thought. He was one of the few people who knew the whole story of how Eve had stolen the documents from his safe and given them to his American rival, who'd promptly released them to the press with all sorts of nasty insinuations. Roark was undoubtedly wondering why, instead of ripping her head off for nearly ruining his billion-dollar company, Talos had proposed that she become his wife.

Roark wasn't much of a talker—the two men had become friends over mutually beneficial business deals in New York and the occasional Knicks basketball game—but any moment he might say something to give it away.

Once Eve realized their past wasn't as rosy as he'd implied, she would never agree to marry him today. And she'd already had her first memory. The clock was ticking. The rest might come tumbling down at any moment. She could get her memory back, then all would be lost. His revenge. His child's name. He had to marry her as soon as possible. Now, before she remembered everything and ran away again, this time taking his baby with her.

"Yes, we're getting married today," Talos confirmed. "And we have additional good news," he said evenly. "We're having a baby."

"Oh," Roark said, then, *"Oh."* He cleared his throat, then suddenly smiled, as if it all made sense now.

A great time to leave. "So if you'll excuse us, we'll be on our way…."

"On your way!" Roark shook his head, clapping Talos heartily on the shoulder. "I wouldn't hear of it. Come down to Tuscany, man. Just three hours' drive from here. I was just headed back home."

"But it's your anniversary," Eve blurted out. "We couldn't possibly intrude."

"Nonsense." He grinned. "I'll call Lia. She hasn't planned an event for ages, since she's been home with the babies. She'll love the excuse for an impromptu party. And she's been wanting a chance to show off the new place since we finished rebuilding the castle…"

"A castle?" Eve breathed. "In Tuscany?"

"Yes. The oldest part is the medieval walls around the rose garden. Particularly beautiful in September. 'Season of mists and mellow fruitfulness,' and all that," he added, looking a bit embarrassed as he glanced down at the package in his arms.

"Keats," she said in surprise.

"Lia loves poetry," he sighed. He held up the wrapped package. "It's a first edition."

Eve shot Talos an imploring look. "It all sounds lovely."

A romantic wedding? With his friends in attendance?

"Absolutely not," Talos said firmly. "We're fine with a quick visit to fill out the paper-work here."

Leaning against his chest, Eve reached her arms up over his neck and looked back at him pleadingly. "Oh please, Talos. I would far rather have a real wedding with some of your friends then just with strangers." She paused and suddenly looked wistful. "With no friends and no wedding party, it wouldn't seem quite real."

No, it wouldn't, Talos thought crossly. And that was just the point. This marriage *wasn't* real. It was a means to an end.

"But I understand," she said with a sigh.

"You don't want to bother your friends on their anniversary." She brightened. "Perhaps we could wait a few days, plan something here in Venice and invite them."

"All right," Talos said through clenched teeth. He would lose this battle to win the war.

"All right?" she repeated.

"We'll wed in Tuscany."

"Oh, thank you!" she cried, whirling around in his arms to embrace him. "You're so good to me!"

"I'll get my car," Roark said.

"No." Holding her in his arms, Talos looked over her head at Roark. "My men will sort out your car. We'll take my plane. There must be no delay."

"I understand." Glancing between the two of them with an amused grin, his friend gave a snort. "I've felt that way myself, too." He pulled out his cell phone. "I'll tell Lia we're on our way."

Eve had never expected when she woke up that morning that today would be her wedding day. Or that she would get married in a castle in Tuscany.

The beautiful Lia Navarre, called *Contessa* by her housekeeper, had immediately taken Eve under her wing. She'd treated her like a dear friend, even though they'd apparently met only once or twice before. When Eve had nervously told her about her amnesia, Lia had only laughed and said she thought amnesia would be an asset in any marriage.

"Believe me," she'd added dryly, "there are a few things about my own marriage I wouldn't mind forgetting."

Eve had watched in awe as Lia simultaneously arranged for a designer to bring six wedding dresses into the bright morning room and organized flower arrangements over the phone, all as she chattered in Italian with her three-year-old daughter and nursed her new baby son to sleep in her arms.

"I hope to be a mother with half your skill," Eve said wistfully as the wedding designer helped her try on yet another dress. She watched Lia tuck her sleeping baby into a nearby bassinet. "You do everything so well, and all at the same time."

Lia looked up with a snicker. "It might look that way, but believe me, I always wonder if

I'm doing enough, or if I'm even doing it right. I'm sure you'll do much better." She tilted her head at Eve. "You know, I never knew you very well, but something about you always confused me."

"What?"

"You've cultivated this image as a party girl, but the time I worked with you on a charity fundraiser, I was shocked at your hard work and drive. You are the most determined person I've ever met, but you just don't let on. You hide it. Why?"

Eve blinked at her, then frowned, turning away with a sigh. "I don't know what to think. Talos described me differently. And now according to you, I'm hardworking and driven? It's like I'm two different people!"

Lia looked at her thoughtfully. "Sometimes we show different sides of ourselves to people for a reason."

"Like what?"

"Oh, I don't know. From a desire to please. From something to hide or something to gain. Oh, this one is lovely." Zipping up Eve's dress, Lia stepped back with a critical eye, then nodded with satisfaction. "Perfect." She looked down at her three-year-old daughter. "Do you like it, Ruby?"

The little girl nodded, her eyes big.

"What do you think?" Lia asked Eve.

Eve looked into the large gilded mirror across the room. The dress was in simple cream-colored silk, cut to accentuate the swell of her breasts and her lush body, falling softly over her belly. Her hair looked glossy and dark, brushing the edges of her pale, bare shoulders. Her blue eyes shone back at her.

Her throat suddenly hurt too much to speak, so she just nodded.

"This is the one," Lia told the designer, who happily started pinning the hem.

"I'm the flower girl," Ruby intoned solemnly to Eve.

"Thank you so much," Eve told her with a big smile. But as Lia positioned a veil over her chignon, Eve saw herself in the mirror and her heart pounded in her chest.

In one hour, she would be married to a man she still barely knew. A man she'd only really known for the last few days.

But I'm carrying his child, she argued with herself. And when he kissed her, he'd managed to brush aside all her nervousness, all her fears. Something about his kiss was magic. And tonight, he would be kissing her again.

More than just kissing her.

Tonight, their wedding night, he would take her to bed and make love to her.

A hot shiver went over her body, and suddenly, she could think of nothing else. All her questions went out the window. All she could think about was the bed that waited for them at the end of the aisle.

What would it feel like when Talos made love to her?

If it was half as wonderful as the kiss had been, she feared she might die of ecstatic joy.

"I hope you'll be very happy, Eve," Lia said to her softly, and there were suddenly tears in her eyes. "Marriage turns romance into love that lasts forever. It creates a family."

A family. Just what Eve wanted more than anything in the world. She nodded, her heart in her throat.

It seemed scant minutes later when, holding freshly cut orange-red roses that matched the blush on her cheeks, she stepped out of the Italian castle into a Tuscan fairyland.

Sunset was falling over the vineyard and green rolling hills. Outside on the covered terrace a million lights drifted from the ceiling, tangled in wisteria. Next to the terrace she saw an old medieval stone wall, overgrown with roses.

The fairy lights sparkled over her head as she stepped onto the stone floor in her simple white sandals. A musician sitting in the back played the first notes on a guitar, accompanied by a flute. All so simple and so magical.

Then she saw Talos.

He was waiting for her at the other end of the terrace. On one side of him stood a friend of Lia's, the mayor of a nearby town who'd agreed to conduct the hastily arranged civil ceremony. On his other side stood his friend Roark. Eve saw the man's face light up at the sight of Lia and their little girl walking ahead in a sweet, frothy cotton dress. At her mother's urging, little Ruby tossed rose petals haphazardly in Eve's path.

Roark picked up his daughter with delighted praise when she reached the end of the aisle. His smile widened as he met his wife's eyes. Seeing their love for each other, as Lia held their plump baby son who looked so dapper in his little suit, Eve's heart stopped in her chest. *This was just what she wanted.*

A life like this.

A love like this.

But when she looked back at her bridegroom with a joyful smile, his expression stopped her cold.

His gaze was dark. Full of heat and fire. But there was something else. Something she didn't understand that frightened her.

The guitar music suddenly trailed off, and she realized that she'd stopped walking halfway down the aisle. With a deep breath, telling herself she was being silly, she started walking again.

Stop acting like a scared virgin! she chided herself.

When she reached the waiting men, Talos pulled her veil up over her head. She looked up at him with a shy smile.

He didn't return it. Instead, his gaze burned through her, incinerating every drop of blood and bone inside her body. As if they were already in bed.

The mayor began to speak, but his accented

words faded into the background. The Navarres disappeared. So did Tuscany, along with the fairy lights and poetry of the mists.

There was only Talos.

His heat.

His fire.

She was dimly aware of repeating the mayor's words, of hearing Talos's deep voice beside her. He slipped a big diamond ring over her finger, then kissed her softly, brushing his mouth against hers.

And just like that—they were man and wife.

CHAPTER SEVEN

FROM the moment Talos saw her in the wedding dress, so lovely and sweet with her shy, happy smile, an earthquake went through his soul.

Eve wore a simple, modest cream-colored wedding dress, with her dark hair beneath a light veil, and she held flame-colored roses in her unmanicured hands. There was no artifice about her. Just beauty. And innocence.

In the brief kiss he gave her after they were wed, his soul trembled within his body. He knew he was on a razor's edge of seducing this beautiful woman, whose fire had once burned him so badly, but who now seemed to shine like the first spring sun after a long, gray winter.

His throat choked as he pulled away from the brief kiss.

Eve, his lying ex-mistress, his hated enemy, was now his wife.

Her big blue eyes shone up at him with such hope and joy, the color of bluebells and violets. He could almost feel the sunlight when he touched her. His longing for her was no longer just about lust, but something more. He longed for her warmth. He could almost hear the laughter of children—his children—bounding through a brightly lit meadow amid cascading sunlight in her innocent promise of happiness.

Lies, he told himself harshly. The woman in front of him, the woman he'd just married, did not really exist.

His hands clenched into fists. She made him want something more. She made him want things he'd never had.

A family.

A home.

This was even more insidious than her earlier betrayal. This kind, loving version of Eve was just an illusion. If he ever allowed himself to care for her, if he ever allowed himself to trust, he would be the biggest fool to walk the earth.

Because as soon as she regained her memory, this woman would disappear. And any day now, she would become the treacherous, selfish woman he remembered.

During the wedding dinner after the ceremony, he watched Eve as she held the baby and entertained three-year-old Ruby. Talos couldn't take his eyes off his bride's radiant beauty—or stop wondering at her generous spirit. The dinner was deliberately simple, homemade pasta and wine from the Navarres' own vintage.

Toward the end of the dinner, Roark and Lia toasted their anniversary with champagne in a private moment, while Eve, still dressed in her simple wedding gown, cuddled their sleeping baby and kept the little girl entertained with charming fairy tales made up out of the air.

What a mother she would make, Talos found himself thinking as he watched her. *What a wife she would make.*

Against his will, his gaze fell upon the neckline and bodice of her gown. His eyes traced her creamy skin, the lush breasts plumped forward as she leaned over to pick a toy from the stone floor.

He wanted Eve so much it hurt. He ached

to caress her. His body tightened painfully, his hand gripping the crystal goblet of red wine.

"Talos?" With a questioning look, Eve placed her small, slender hand over his. Her caress and the tender expression of her impossibly beautiful shining face caused a shock wave to go through him.

And he suddenly realized that this sweetly loving woman was more dangerous than the seductive, sexy mistress had ever been.

He wanted her. All of her.

In his bed.

In his life.

He hungered for the dream she offered him. Hungered for her illusion to be true. Most of all, he hungered for the bedroom he knew awaited them in the guest wing of the castle, festooned with rose petals, candles and soft sheets.

No, he told himself furiously. He couldn't give in!

Ripping his hand away from Eve's, he crashed the crystal goblet down so hard on the table that it cracked, exploding red wine all over the wood like blood.

Three-year-old Ruby cried out in shock.

Roark and Lia, who'd been cuddled at the other end of the table with intimate, private laughter, looked up with a gasp.

"Sorry," Talos muttered. He rose to his feet. "Sorry."

Staring at their faces, he backed away.

"What is it?" Eve whispered. "What's wrong?"

He had the sudden image of her pale, frightened face.

"We have to go," he ground out. He focused on his friends behind her. Roark and Lia had gone far beyond the call of duty to create a fairytale wedding for them with only a few hours' notice, though they had their own responsibilities with their young children; though they had their own anniversary to celebrate. "Thanks for arranging our wedding."

"Surely you're not leaving?" Lia demanded. "I prepared a guest room for you…"

Yes, he'd seen the honeymoon suite, and he wanted no part of it.

"Sorry," he bit out. "We can't stay."

Lia's eyes widened. Talos knew he was being incredibly callous but he would explain to Roark later. His old friend would understand, and he'd make his amends to his wife. All Talos knew was that he couldn't stay for another hour in this romantic place so filled with happy dreams that for him would always be lies.

Talos broke out in a cold sweat.

He had to get out of here.

He had to end this.

He'd won his objective. Eve was his wife. His war was half won. Now all he had to do was make her regain her memory. Now. Before the temptation was too much.

Before Eve finished what she'd started three months ago, and finally crushed him into ashes and dust.

He abruptly turned on his heel, whirling away from the terrace with its overhanging wisteria and fairy lights gleaming in the night.

"Talos? Talos!" he heard his wife cry after him as he strode into the villa, but he didn't look back. Instead, he opened his cell phone and started to bark out orders.

Eve had started this war three months ago.

Now he would finish it.

"Mrs. Xenakis, the plane will be landing shortly."

Eve woke up blearily to discover a pretty

brunette flight attendant standing over her, holding a tray. Sitting up straight in the white leather chair, she rubbed her eyes, feeling sweaty and disoriented. She smoothed her wedding dress with her hands, but it didn't help. The cream-colored silk was wrinkled and wilted.

Just like her wedding day.

Eve's head was still spinning. One moment, she'd been a happy bride, pledging her fealty and her faith to the father of her unborn child.

The next, Talos had been dragging her from the castle, pushing her into a car that took them back to the private airport. They'd left without even properly thanking Lia and Roark for the lovely wedding they'd created. Talos had forced her to leave the cheerfully decorated table with its flowers and lights, the homemade pasta and bread. They'd fled the celebration as if they were thieves in the night, rudely abandoning their kind hosts without explanation as Talos herded her onto his private plane.

There, he'd utterly ignored her and refused to answer any of her questions. He'd gone to the other side of the large cabin to a desk that was as far away from Eve as possible. He'd barked an order to a flight attendant for a shot of Scotch whisky—then hadn't even drunk it. He'd just taken a deep sniff of the amber-colored Scotch before handing it back, telling the flight attendant to pour it out.

Had he gone mad?

Or had she?

He'd spent the rest of the short flight working on his computer. Bewildered and hurt, Eve had fallen asleep staring out the small window of the plane, watching the lights of the Italian coastline disappear over the black emptiness of the Adriatic.

Now, as she looked out the small round window, she saw small clusters of lights amid the darkness, like scattered stars in the night. "Where are we?"

"Beginning our descent into Athens, madam."

"Athens!" Eve cried. "How long was I sleeping?"

The brunette gave a sympathetic smile. "Almost two hours."

Two hours. She glanced over at her new

husband, who was still sitting at his desk, staring at his laptop screen with hard eyes.

Maybe he has work to do, she tried to tell herself. Urgent, unavoidable work that he was desperate to finish so they could properly enjoy our honeymoon.

But she wasn't completely comforted by her explanation. Not when he'd turned so cold and unresponsive from the moment he'd become her husband.

It was almost as if he were angry at her. But that didn't make sense. Hadn't he come to London, desperate to find her? Hadn't he proposed marriage when he found out she was pregnant with his child? Hadn't he spent days passionately, tenderly convincing her to marry him?

She'd finally agreed to be his wife. They'd had a romantic, perfect wedding. So why was he suddenly acting like a man who despised the thought of her existence?

She rubbed her head wearily, causing more tendrils to tumble from her chignon. It didn't make sense. Was her confusion caused by her amnesia? Why couldn't she understand him?

The flight attendant carefully set down

her tray on a nearby table. "Mr. Xenakis thought you might wish to have a snack before we land."

Eve saw a nice selection of cut fruits and bread and cheeses, as well as sparkling water and juices. She glanced at her husband across the cabin. "He didn't want to join me?" she said, trying—and failing—to keep the hurt from her voice.

The flight attendant gave her a sympathetic look. "Sorry, madam."

As the flight attendant departed, Eve tried furiously to think, to understand. Talos couldn't have married her for her money, since her fortune, nice as it was, was just a fraction of his. Then why?

Because she was pregnant with his baby? He'd said he wanted to give their baby a name. Was that the only reason?

No, she told herself desperately. He'd married her because he loved her.

Although he'd never said the words, had he?

She drank the water and ate the fruit, though she had no appetite as the plane landed. Talos, in spite of her hurt glances, continued to ignore her long after the plane had landed on the tarmac. After the plane door opened and they came down the stairs, she took a deep breath.

Athens at midnight.

His assistants and various bodyguards were waiting for him on the tarmac, along with two cars to whisk their entourage into the city. They were swiftly and seamlessly escorted through customs. Within minutes, she was seated next to her husband in the back of a black Bentley as the chauffeur drove them on the six-lane highway into the city.

She stared at him until he finally looked at her.

"Talos, why are you acting like this?" she asked quietly.

"Like what?" he demanded.

"Like a jerk."

Clenching his jaw, he looked out at the darkness of the passing city. "I'm sorry if you are so needy and insecure that you feel you must be the center of my attention at every moment," he said in a low voice. "But unlike you, I am not content just to sponge off an income earned by someone else. Unlike you, I own a business and must run it. The fact that we're married does not mean I intend to spend my every hour worshipping you."

She gaped at him, openmouthed.

He'd ignored her for the hours since their wedding, he'd rudely insulted their friends, he'd dragged her from Italy to Greece without explanation…and now he was trying to make her think *she* was the one with the problem?

Biting back an angry retort, she took a deep breath and tried to see things from his position, tried to see if there was a possibility she was being unreasonable.

Nope.

Clasping her hands together, she took another deep, calming breath. She was his wife now. She wanted to be loving and understanding. They were on their honeymoon. She didn't want to start a fight over something so small as his strangely irritated mood.

On the other hand, she wasn't a doormat, and he'd best learn that right now.

"Of course I understand you must work," she tried in her kindest, most understanding voice. "But that doesn't explain why you've been so cold to me all night. Or why you dragged us away from Tuscany." She swallowed. "After your friends went to such trouble, we could have at least spent the night there…"

His dark eyes stabbed daggers at her. "It didn't interest me."

She flushed, feeling humiliated as she sat unwanted in her wrinkled, sad little wedding dress. All night long she'd felt a thrilling ache, a twitter in her belly as she'd imagined their wedding night, thinking of him kissing her, yearning to experience what it felt like when he made love to her.

Apparently the same thought interested him not at all.

"Why are you pushing me away like this?" she whispered. "You've done it since the moment I became your wife. Do you—do you regret marrying me?"

He stared at her for a moment, then turned away, pulling his laptop from his leather briefcase. "We'll be home soon."

"Why are you acting as if you suddenly hate me?"

He closed the laptop with a loud snap. "I'm not going to discuss this right now, Eve."

"Then when?"

His phone rang. He looked down at it before

he gave her a narrowed glance. "You'll know everything soon enough." Turning from her, he opened the phone and barked, "Xenakis."

As he spoke on the phone in Greek, she glanced down at the bright diamond ring on her finger. It sparkled at her, sharp facets without a soul. With a sense of foreboding, she looked up through the window at the darkly sprawling city of ancient white buildings and olive trees surrounded by cragged mountains.

Why would Talos marry her if he intended to treat her like this?

She placed her hand on her belly, where their baby was growing inside her. Her stomach was starting to grow more rounded beneath the swell of her breasts.

I wouldn't have given him my virginity unless he was worthy of my love, she told herself.

How do you know? the gleefully sadistic whisper asked. *How do you know what sort of person you are?*

Shut up, she told the voice sharply. *I know.*

But it was too late. Fear had already crept inside her, a dull poison of fear she could neither dispel nor reason away.

She hadn't wanted to marry him so

quickly. She'd tried to resist, to delay. But he'd kept insisting. Courting her. Wooing her.

He'd been so loving. So patient. So *perfect*.

And then he'd kissed her on the bridge in Venice, and all of her objections had been swept away in a storm of fierce, blind desire unlike anything she could possibly withstand. His embrace had stolen her strength away, leaving her abject in his arms, with no choice but to surrender to his will.

Now, it seemed there would be no more kisses.

Had she made a horrible mistake marrying Talos?

You're right to be afraid, he'd said with that strange light in his eyes.

Was it possible he'd married her just because she was pregnant with his child? Or for some other, darker reason of his own?

It couldn't be for love—not when he acted like this!

The Bentley pulled up outside an elegant fin de siècle building, nine stories high, on an imposing square in the center of the city. Talos got out without a backward glance. For the first time, he allowed the chauffeur to assist her from the car.

Stepping out on the sidewalk, Eve looked up at the building and the Acropolis, lit up on the high crag above them. She nearly jumped at Talos's voice behind her.

"Beautiful, isn't it?"

She whirled around to see him looking at her with a cruel amusement.

"Yes," she said over the lump in her throat. Beautiful and haughty and a bit savage, just like him.

As his driver and the bellman dealt with the luggage, Talos stepped closer to her. He was so close she could feel his breath, feel the warmth of his strong body beneath his clothes. Leaning forward, not touching her, he whispered, "You'll love the view from the penthouse."

She shivered as he leaned forward.

"It's where you first gave yourself to me," he whispered in her ear, brushing his lips against her tender flesh. "For weeks, we never left our bed."

He stood away from her, his dark eyes gleaming. And though she tried to hide the reaction he'd caused in her, she knew he could read her tension. Her desire.

It infuriated her. Defiantly, she lifted her chin. "Well, I hope you enjoyed it, because it won't happen again."

His eyes darkened at her challenge. He grabbed her hand, and though she tried to pull it away, he would not release her. As the staff and bodyguards trailed them, they went through the exquisite lobby and up the elevator.

It was only when they were alone in the large penthouse condo that he released her.

She rubbed her wrist, staring at him. "Why were you so determined to marry me right away, Talos?" she demanded. "Why? I want the truth right now!"

"The truth?" he said tersely. "What a novel idea where you're concerned."

She pushed aside the little pain at his jab. "Was it because I'm pregnant?"

He looked away. "I will always protect my child."

Pain went through her. Not love, then. Nothing to do with love. "If it was only for the baby's sake, why did you lie?" she said hoarsely. "Why did you say you loved me?"

"I never lied to you." His mouth pressed into a hard line as he stared down at her. "I said I wished to marry you and give the baby a name. Both of which are true."

She shook her head, fighting unbidden tears. "You made me believe you loved me," she whispered. "You tricked me into marriage. Don't you have any sense of honor—any honor at all?"

"Honor!" Their faces were an inch apart as he looked at her with a sneer. "You accuse *me* of dishonor!"

She felt suddenly afraid, trapped, his hard body over hers, his strong hands like shackles on her wrists.

Then she felt his breath on her skin. Heard his breathing change as the mood between them electrified, changing from anger to something else. His grip on her wrists tightened, his gaze dropping to her mouth. Her heart stopped in her chest, then began to flutter wildly. *Thum-thumm. Thumm-thum.* She tingled from her lips to her breasts down to her deepest core.

With a savage intake of breath, he dropped her wrists.

Turning away from her, he walked down the hall. His footsteps echoed heavily against the marble floor. A moment later, he returned with something flimsy and silver that sparkled in his hands.

"Get dressed," he said, his lip curling with scorn. He tossed the silvery fabric at her. "Wear that."

For a moment, she just stared at him, holding the sequined fabric close to her chest. Behind him, the floor-to-ceiling windows revealed the majestic Acropolis, lit up with brilliant lights on the cragged mountain like a torch above the city. She could see the white stone buildings below them, interspersed with palm and olive trees. Her heart was still pounding, her brain in a fog from his closeness a moment ago.

Then she held up the tiny cocktail dress, metallic and shiny and silver. It was dead sexy—and hard. Just like all the clothes she'd given away in Venice.

"No." She lifted her chin. "I told you. I don't want to dress like that anymore."

"You'll do what I tell you."

"I'm your wife, not your slave."

Crossing the room in three strides of his powerful legs, he grabbed her by the shoulders. "You'll obey me, or—"

She tossed her hair back, revealing her neck as she glared at him. "Or what?"

Their eyes locked, held. She heard the quickening of his breath, the gasp of her own.

He wanted to kiss her. She knew it. She could feel it.

But abruptly, he released her. His expression became a mask and he looked almost bored as he glanced at his expensive platinum watch.

"You'd best hurry. We leave in ten minutes." He paused at the door. "Look your best, won't you?" he said coolly. "A special friend of yours will be at the party."

"Party? What party? What special friend?"

But he left her without answer, leaving her to change her clothes alone.

Alone, she thought bitterly.

She hadn't even known what that word really meant until she became a wife.

CHAPTER EIGHT

He'd been too gentle with her, Talos thought grimly.

As he sat next to Eve on the short drive west toward the nearby neighborhood of Monastiráki, he ignored her angry, shallow huffs of breath beside him. He'd been tempted to tell her everything in the penthouse, but he'd held back for the sake of his child in her belly. For fear the shock would cause miscarriage.

Ridiculous, he thought now, grinding his teeth. Eve was too strong for that. His ex-mistress—his *wife,* he corrected himself—was as hard as steel. A force of nature. Ridiculous to worry about an emotional shock causing injury to their unborn child, when the Eve he'd known had no feelings whatsoever!

But in mere moments, she would finally remember everything—and be forced to admit everything—when she saw her lover.

Clenching his jaw, he stared out the window. The Bentley drove past the dark alley, not too far from Constitution Square where he'd committed his one and only criminal act. At fifteen, two months after his mother had died, he'd smashed the window of an expensive car. It had not gone as planned. The owner of the car had stumbled upon Talos on the sidewalk, holding the ripped-out car stereo in his hands.

Talos hadn't tried to deny his crime. He'd openly confessed and, with as much charm as his self-taught English could muster, suggested he'd done the man a favor. "I think a different brand of stereo might suit you better." Then, with a bowed head, he'd waited for him to call the police.

Instead, Dalton Hunter had hired him on the spot. "Our Athens office could use a kid like you," he'd said with a laugh. And Talos had soon found himself the new messenger and office boy for the American CEO's worldwide shipping corporation.

From that day, remembering his crime with shame, Talos had been obsessed with justice.

After climbing the corporate ladder and making some lucky investments, he'd made his first million by the age of twenty-four. The father who'd abandoned his mother when she was pregnant with Talos had read about him in the newspaper and had contacted him.

Not to ask for money, he'd said. Just for a visit.

Talos had refused even to speak with him.

A man earned the circumstances of his life. He got what he deserved.

And Yiorgos had caused Talos's mother financial and emotional distress which had ultimately led to her early death. The man might share Talos's DNA, but that was all. Dalton Hunter had been far more of a father to him than that man had ever been.

At least so Talos had thought until eleven years ago, when Dalton had turned out to be utterly corrupt.

But when it came to corruption, one woman had beaten them all.

He glanced at Eve. She looked coldly beautiful in the tiny silver cocktail dress and stiletto heels. Her lips were scarlet as blood, her eyelashes black as night against her white skin. Just like the ruthless mistress he remembered. As if nothing had changed.

Wasn't that what he'd wanted?

The car stopped in front of an old white building, once part of a thirteenth-century monastery, now an art gallery nightclub started by a friend. Talos climbed out of the car, straightening the cuff links on the white shirt beneath his black blazer as he waited. The chauffeur opened Eve's door, and she walked up to him on stiletto heels with a graceful swing of her hips.

"What is it?" she said acidly, tossing her head. Her lip curled. "Aren't you happy with how I look?"

Was he happy? He looked down at her. Eve's glossy dark hair had been pulled back into a severe ponytail that revealed the perfection of her bone structure and her creamy skin. Silver earrings dangled against her long neck. A tight silver cuff coiled up her bare arm in the shape of a snake.

She was a cold goddess.

Breathtaking.

Powerful.

"You'll do," he said evenly. He yanked her toward the door.

The asymmetrical straps of her silver dress hung askew on her shoulders, apparently threatening to fall at any moment to reveal her amazing breasts. He knew it was only a cunning artifice of design, but as they walked into the crumbling white building, and he heard the tap-tap-tap of her six-inch-high silver stiletto heels beside him, he watched men get whiplash from turning their heads to gawk at her.

Eve lifted her chin stonily, pretending not to notice. She was graceful, full of dignity. But he could feel her simmering fury rising from her beautiful body in waves.

Talos glared at them with a snarl curling his lip.

In the past, he'd been arrogantly proud to have the woman that every other man wanted. He'd taken it as his due—other, lesser men always envied what Talos possessed.

That had changed in Venice. And now, when he saw men craning their heads to look at her, pure rage washed over him.

Why? Why was he so angry and posses-sive? Because she was his wife?

Wife in name only, he told himself fiercely. And tonight, he would finally get his revenge. Once she saw her old love, she would remember everything. He would see her face crumple when she realized how she'd been caught.

"Talos!" The hostess, a thirtysomething socialite married to a Greek tycoon three times her age, came forward to greet him with a big smile. "What a wonderful surprise, darling! Your assistant sent your regrets. And—" She looked at Eve and her eyes went wide. "Oh my goodness. Eve Craig. I didn't expect—I never thought you might—"

"Is Skinner here?" Talos interrupted.

The woman had been staring at Eve in consternation, but now she whirled to face Talos, biting her lip. "I heard you were in Australia. I never would have invited him otherwise," she implored. "Please, darling, I don't want trouble!"

"Don't worry, Agata," he replied, gritting his teeth into a smile. "We're just going to have a bit of a chat."

She exhaled. "I'll hold you to that." She eyed Eve, then as photographers came close to take their picture, put her arm around her and smiled before giving her an air kiss. "I didn't realize you and Talos were still an item, Eve darling."

"We are," Eve replied coldly, then folded her arms as she waited for Talos.

Clenching his jaw, he looked downstairs over the railing. The cavernous white stone building was decorated with candles and modern-day icons looking up mournfully from gilded frames. All of the international party set was here to celebrate Agata's twenty-ninth birthday—her third such party, if he recalled correctly. Suddenly, across the room, past the dance floor and the colorfully painted wooden bar with Agata's hand-selected shirtless bartenders, Talos saw his rival—Jake Skinner.

Talos glanced quickly at Eve, waiting for her to see the tall American tycoon. Instead, she was staring up at him with an angry frown, searing him with her violet-blue eyes.

"Enjoying yourself?" she said acidly. "Is this why you married me? So you could parade me at parties like your little doll?"

"I can do whatever I want with you," he said coldly.

Cupping her bare arm, he steered her down the stairs and straight across the room to Jake Skinner. With a flicker of his eyes, Talos looked between them, waiting for recognition to cross Eve's beautiful face at the sight of the man she'd dated before Talos. The man who held her loyalty. *The man she loved.*

Whirling around, the rugged American playboy nearly gasped at the sight of Talos. He looked around nervously for the exits. "Xenakis, it's a public place. Don't even think about—"

"Relax. I'm here to enjoy myself."

Skinner visibly exhaled.

"No hard feelings, right?" he said in a jocular voice. "I only gave that document to the press because it seemed as if you were breaking the law."

That, plus he'd hoped to gain massive profit for his own shareholders, Talos thought. He bared his teeth into a smile. "Of course, I understand. For all you knew, I might have been guilty. And no one—" he

looked down at Eve "—should remain un-
punished for their crimes."

Eve's brow furrowed as she stared up at
him, as if trying to understand the meaning
beneath his words. She didn't seem to have
any interest in Jake Skinner whatsoever.

Why wasn't this working? Skinner was
the love of her life. He had to be. There
could be no other reason for her cold-
blooded betrayal of him in June. So why
wasn't she reacting at the sight of him?
Why wasn't she crying out his name,
gasping out her sudden memory, turning to
Talos in horror and realizing she'd been ir-
revocably caught?

Clenching his jaw, Talos turned to give his
rival a hard smile. "And just to show you
there's no hard feelings, Skinner, here's a
little peace offering."

He shoved Eve toward him. She stumbled
in surprise, nearly tripping on her six-inch
stiletto heels.

The American's jaw dropped, and his voice
hit a high octave as he gasped, "Your peace
offering is—Eve?"

"Forget it, you bastard," Eve said furiously, whirling back to face Talos. "I won't do it. I won't even dance with him—"

"You will."

She sucked in her breath, and for a moment he thought she meant to slap his face.

Then she straightened her spine with graceful dignity.

"What a lovely idea," she said coldly, turning to Skinner with a smile on her scarlet lips. "Shall we dance?"

"Yes," the man breathed. "Oh, yes."

His eyes held such flagrant desire that Talos's hands clenched into fists at his sides. He watched as his business rival collected his wife, taking her hand in his own, and escorted her to the dance floor.

And as the music started, Talos was unable to look away.

Eve was a beautiful dancer. She always had been. Every step she took caused the silvery sequined dress to move in waves over her luscious body. Without touching the other man, she moved slowly, sensually, in front of him, holding her arms over her head. The bottom of the dress barely brushed her thighs as she swayed her hips, closing her eyes.

Jake Skinner, along with nearly every other man on the dance floor, had stopped to gape at her, slack-jawed. The other women on the floor, many of whom were also very beautiful, noticed their men had frozen in place and they, too, turned to glare.

With her eyes still closed, Eve swayed to the music.

She moved like the seductive siren of every man's hungry dreams.

Talos suddenly felt as though he was choking for air—or dying of thirst. Grabbing a martini from a waiter who'd stopped in front of him to stare at his wife, Talos gulped it all down at once.

Then he looked back at Eve. Every man in the room was staring at her. He felt a sudden stabbing pain against his palm and looked down, realizing he'd just shattered the martini glass in his hand.

"Me singkorite!" With a gasp, a nearby waiter turned and scurried to grab a broom.

"Oriste." Agata was suddenly standing next to him. She held out a small towel.

Talos took it. *"Efkharisto."*

"You're wasting your time with her," she

said quietly, nodding toward Eve. "You're going to get hurt."

"You're wrong." Talos wiped the blood off his hand with the towel. The cuts weren't deep. "She can't hurt me."

But he knew he was lying. Eve had cut him to the bone long ago.

He watched her across the room, dancing with her eyes closed, her arms swaying over her head. His lust for Eve cut far deeper than any blade. Like every other man in the room, he wanted her so badly that every nerve in his body vibrated with her music. And after three months of constant longing, an increasingly frustrated desire had left him frayed like fabric, falling apart at the edges.

After being so close to her, courting her, of having her in his bed but not being able to touch her, he was going mad. *Lust for her was killing him.*

He'd been so certain that coming to the party tonight would cause Eve to regain her memory and return to the cruel, grasping seductress he remembered. And she had—but in a way he'd never expected.

She was taunting him.

Watching her move and sway, he swallowed his lust, his whole body in a hot sweat. As the song ended, Talos felt, rather than heard, the low deep growl of every man in the place wanting Eve. Felt the press of male footsteps and bodies leaning toward her.

As if coming out of a trance, Eve slowly opened her eyes.

Talos saw Jake Skinner reach for her as the dance ended. Reaching with his hands, with his hungry eyes, with his mouth—

Suddenly, Talos found himself across the room and in the middle of the dance floor.

He pushed his rival aside.

"Stay—away—from—my—wife!"

He drew back in shock. "Your wife?" Skinner gasped. He backed away, his face turning white. "You're married?"

Eve just tilted her head quizzically. "As a matter of fact, we are." She tossed Talos a look through narrowed eyes. "I didn't know you cared."

"I care," he ground out. Tightening his jaw, Talos looked at his American rival. Every muscle was taut with the control it took not to attack the other man. "Stay away from my wife," he said again in a low voice.

Skinner looked between them quickly. What he saw in Talos's face must have convinced him, because he turned and ran, pushing his way past the party guests, nearly knocking over their hostess in his haste.

Talos felt the eyes of the whole room upon them. So much for telling Agata that he wouldn't make a scene.

"Happy birthday," he told Agata abruptly. "Thanks for the party."

Lacing his fingers through Eve's, he escorted her out of the building. Only when they were on the sidewalk and the cooling night air hit their skin, did he turn to her.

"You little fool," he bit out. "What were you thinking with that little show?"

But she clearly wasn't going to let him railroad her.

"Isn't that what you wanted?" she retorted furiously, tossing her head. "Isn't this who you want me to be?" She blinked back sudden tears. "And you think just because you don't want me, you can pass me off to your friends—"

He pushed toward her, backing her into the darkness of the rough, rubbish-strewn alley.

"You think I don't want you?" he said dangerously.

When her heels hit the stone wall, she stopped, lifting her chin. Her eyes shimmered in the moonlight as she matched him toe-to-toe, holding her ground.

"I think you're a liar," she said hoarsely. "You lured me into marrying you under false pretenses, and now you want to punish me for some reason. I don't know why, but I was a fool to trust your words, your lying kisses. I can't believe I ever let you touch me. I never will again—"

He cut her off with a kiss, pushing her back against the rough stone, holding her wrists like shackles against the wall. He spread her lips wide, thrusting his tongue inside her mouth, deepening the kiss until she sagged in his arms. *Until she started to kiss him back.*

The moment he felt her lips move against his, as she matched his fire with her own, a surge of reckless joy went through him that he could not control.

He was going to take her right here in the

alley. Against the wall. Damn the consequences.

He would possess her now, even if he died for it.

Eve's breath came in little gasps as he slowly kissed up her neck, his arms tracing up and down her naked skin.

"Why are you doing this?" she whispered. Feeling his mouth on her sent sparks down her body until she thought she might forget to breathe. "I did what you wanted. Why are you so angry? Why do you feel possessive because I danced with your friend—exactly as you wanted?"

"Seeing all those other men lusting for you was never what I wanted," he ground out.

"Then why?" she managed as his hands stroked her roughly over the sequins of her dress. "Why are you killing me like this— kissing me one moment then pushing me away the next? As if you hate me? Why are you torturing me?"

His hands stilled. He looked down at her, and the fire in his eyes of a moment before had changed to longing. To confusion. *To pain.*

Staring down at her, he suddenly yanked off his black blazer. Without a word, he wrapped it around her tiny silver dress. The jacket hung long on her, covering her modestly to mid-thigh.

Grabbing the jacket's lapels, he pulled her close. He leaned his head forward, pressing his forehead against hers.

When he spoke, his voice was so low she barely heard his words. "I'm sorry."

And just like that, she exhaled.

He pulled her gently from the alley to the Bentley waiting for them on the street. Without explanation, Talos opened Eve's door and helped her inside. He didn't speak to her in the car—he didn't even look at her.

But he held her hand tightly all the way to his penthouse.

When they arrived at his apartment a few moments later, he helped her out of the car. Still, he held her hand and didn't let go.

She stared up at him in a daze, unable to look away from his darkly handsome face as they crossed the lobby of the elegant nineteenth-century building and went into the elevator. At the door of the penthouse,

Talos unlocked it and turned to her, his face dark with need.

"I should have done this a long time ago."

He lifted her in his arms. His body glowed with warmth and heat she could almost see, burning off his body in waves. Holding her closely, Talos kicked the door open, then kicked it closed behind them.

Crossing the penthouse, with the view of the lit-up Acropolis on the mountain floating high above the night, he gently set her on her feet on the marble floor. Never taking his eyes from hers, he peeled his large black jacket off her shoulders, dropping it to the floor.

She closed her eyes, her breath shortening as she felt him reach behind her head and undo her ponytail. Her hair fell softly against her shoulders in one shake.

She felt his hands run over her body, stroking her over her silvery cocktail dress.

"You're mine, Eve," he whispered. He traced his large hands over her hips, over her slender waist.

He ran his hands back over her whisper-thin silver dress, causing it to slink and move over her body like a caress. She felt his thumbs brush against her breasts, making her nipples harden to agonizing intensity beneath the fabric. Her breasts felt heavy and swollen, swaying as he cupped them reverently in his hands. Her whole body felt tight and hot. She felt dizzy all over, her knees weak.

Her eyes flew open as he knelt at her feet. The room seemed to spin around her as she watched him stroke slowly down her bare legs, from her thighs to the backs of her knees. Massaging her calves, he slowly removed one stiletto heel, then the other, dragging them gently against the tender hollow of her foot. He sent the shoes skidding across the floor.

His gaze locked on hers, hot and dark.

Slowly, he rose back to his feet. Never taking his eyes from hers, he removed his tuxedo tie. He unbuttoned his white shirt, dropping it carelessly to the floor. She had the sudden vision of his bare chest, powerfully muscled and laced with dark hair.

Then he stood naked and powerful in front of her. His olive skin gleamed in the sharp moonlight, which cascaded over the hard planes of his body. Every inch of his muscular body exuded masculine power.

Looking down, she saw how much he wanted her, and she swallowed, afraid of his strength, his size. She was pregnant with his child, and yet with no memory she felt as shy as a virgin.

Murmuring endearments in Greek, he picked Eve up in his arms. Carrying her across the room, he gently set her down on the enormous bed. Stretching her arms above her, he pulled off her little sliver of a gown. Pushing her back against the pillows, he pulled off her panties. And suddenly she was naked in front of him, naked on their bed.

The thought terrified her, but before she could move away, he was on top of her. She felt his hardness against her belly as he slowly kissed her neck, sucking on her earlobes, softly brushing back her hair as he whispered in her ear, "*Ekho sizigho*. My sweet one."

He cupped her breasts together, nuzzling between them, thumbing the nipples until they tightened to agonizing points. He suckled first one, then the other, before moving down her body to kiss her belly. His hands stroked her hips, brushing her thighs before he moved up to kiss her mouth. His kiss was hard, hungry. He wrapped his arms beneath her shoulders, holding her tightly to his body. She gasped as she felt him between her legs, pushing her thighs apart.

A satisfied masculine growl escaped him as he moved his hardness against her slick, wet heat. She twisted beneath him as the low tension built deeper and deeper inside her, making her breath come out in quick little pants, making her body sizzle from her taut nipples to her hot molten core. She was melting for him, melting to nothing, and if he didn't…

He slid inside her with a single deep stroke.

Her back arched. She cried out as he filled her to the hilt, releasing pleasure so deep inside it was almost pain.

He choked out a gasp, closing his eyes as he thrust inside her again, pulling back, riding her hard and slow. Each stab was deeper, spiraling a sweet ecstasy so far inside her that she thought she might be devoured by it.

He spread her wide, splitting her apart. Harder, faster, pain, pleasure. Just four times. Four thrusts, each one deeper and harder than the last.

And she exploded.

CHAPTER NINE

As Talos felt her body tighten, he knew he could not last.

Touching her was heaven. Her skin was even softer than he remembered. She tasted sweet, so sweet. The very first time he slid inside her, he nearly lost control. With every thick thrust he watched her full breasts sway from the force of his possession, and he gasped out each breath. How long had he wanted her?

How had he denied himself for so long?

With each slow thrust inside her, he shattered a little more, until he was coming apart like Venetian stucco falling into the water. His whole body shook with the agony of holding himself back when all he wanted to do was bury himself in her completely, to lose himself in the ecstasy of making love to her. Every nerve was on fire. It had never felt like this before—not even with her.

Three thrusts, and he was shaking with the desperate effort to stay in control. He grunted as he shoved into her roughly, pushing all the way to the hilt in pleasure so great he nearly lost his mind. He heard her soft gasp spread to a scream and felt her shudder as her body convulsed around him. And he could hold back no longer. With a shout, he shoved inside her one last time with a guttural cry, pulsing and spurting inside her.

Spent, he collapsed next to her, pulling her into his arms, holding her tightly.

Now, as he looked at the gray light coming from the windows, he realized it was already morning. They'd slept in each other's arms for at least two hours.

Something he'd never done before.

Oh, they'd slept in bed together, of course, between stretches of nearly constant lovemaking. But he'd never just held her like this, cradling her against his chest as they drowsed.

He felt…contented. *Protective.*

He stared down at her naked beauty. The

white cotton sheets had fallen past her hips. Her skin was lustrous and creamy. Her breasts were heavy and swelling, the tips that he'd suckled so recently now a shade of pink that was the color of deep pink roses. The slight swell of his child in her belly only made her look more feminine, like a goddess of fertility.

He felt himself instantly go hard. He already wanted her again. And not just her body…

How had she changed so much?

How could losing her memory make her into such a different person?

He'd tried to resist her. He had every reason in the world to punish and hurt her. *But he could not.*

Something inside Talos wouldn't let him do it. Even as his exacting soul cried out for justice, he could not hurt her.

There was only one card left to play. One last chance for justice.

He could tell her the truth.

He could take her to the place where she'd betrayed him.

It was his last chance.

Because this new Eve, the woman now

sleeping in his arms, was too beautiful, too real, too vulnerable. Too warm and natural and loving.

He'd counted on her having no defenses. He'd never thought that her innocence would cause him to lose his own defenses.

But sooner or later, Eve would revert to her true self, the cold, cruel, clever siren who'd sold him out for love or money. The woman who would undoubtedly hate their baby because of what the pregnancy did to her perfect figure. The woman who would ignore and neglect her child for her own selfish pursuits.

Who would never want to settle down with any man for long.

His fingers tightened on her as he took a deep breath. He had to end this. *Today*. He had to erase this new woman completely. Before he…before he…

He suddenly heard a strange sound. Frowning, he looked down at the woman in his arms.

For a moment, he heard only the quiet snuffle of her breathing and the sound of morning birds singing outside in the pale blue of dawn.

Then he heard Eve suck in her breath again. And she started to scream.

Cradled in Talos's strong arms, beneath the soft dawn spilling from the windows, Eve hadn't wanted to wake up. She'd pressed her head against his naked chest, relishing the feel of his warm skin laced with dark hair.

His body was so much larger than her own. Snuggled against him in the enormous bed, she'd felt protected. Safe. *Loved.* There was so much about him she still didn't understand. But still, she was falling in love with him all over again.

Drowsy and content, she'd listened to the beat of his heart against her cheek. The beat grew louder, like the sound of heavy footsteps stomping in unison against a hard stone floor. *Step. Step. Step.*

She felt suddenly cold as she looked at the blurry faces around her. Her mother's sobbing face came into sharp focus. She clung to Eve, wailing as they watched her father's coffin pass out of the church on the shoulders of old men. Eve clutched her mother's hands in her own, suddenly terrified that her father's death would cause her to lose both her parents. In the last week, she'd lost her father, their home, their fortune, their reputation. And it was all that man's fault. He'd destroyed her father with all his lies. He'd heartlessly destroyed them all....

Now outside, standing on the frozen grass of the cemetery beside the dark-clothed mourners, she saw the cold March wind blow her mother's black veil back like a dark spirit. She saw her mother stretch her arms toward the coffin as her beloved husband was lowered into the earth, as if she intended to bury herself in the same cold grave....

"No!" Eve screamed. "Please!"

"Eve!" She suddenly felt a man's strong, protective arms around her, his voice anxious as he enveloped her with his warmth. "Wake up. Wake up."

With a choked gasp, Eve opened her eyes. And saw Talos's face.

"What—what is it?"

"You were screaming." He held her tightly, stroking her face, stroking her hair. His dark eyes were full of concern. "Did you have a dream?"

A dream?

Pain racked through her, and suddenly her head was pounding as if her skull had been fractured into pieces. She pushed away from him as tears streamed down her face. For some reason, she suddenly couldn't stand his touch.

"I remembered my father's funeral," she whispered.

She pushed away, standing up, then realized she was naked. She froze, remembering their night together. Remembering how happy she'd been sleeping in his arms...

She took a deep, ragged breath, pushing her hair out of her eyes. "I'll go take a shower." Before he could reply, she added quickly, "Alone."

Talos's eyes darkened. He turned away from her, reaching into his closet. "Fine."

She took a quick shower, trying to wash away the sharp pain of her memory. She quickly dressed in clothes for the hot Greek sun—a pale pink tank top, a short knit skirt and white flat sandals. Brushing her hair, she stared at herself in the mirror.

All these days she'd been so desperate to remember her past. And now...

What if she didn't like what she found?

"Are you hungry?" Talos asked quietly when she came out into the bedroom. "Shall we have a quick breakfast?"

"That sounds fine," she said, careful not to touch him. Anything to get away from this place where, just as she'd found happiness at last, she'd been stabbed with pain.

Talos left his hands stuffed in his jacket pockets as they took the elevator downstairs. He opened the back door of the Bentley and helped her inside. But as he sat next to her on the short drive, he kept his distance. As if there were an invisible wall between them.

To think last night, he'd held her so tightly, whispering endearments to her in Greek, covering her body with hot kisses as he pressed his naked body against hers.

How had everything changed so much since then?

"What else don't I remember?" she whispered. "What if it's all bad? What if it's worse?"

He set his jaw. "What could be worse?"

"What happened to my father?"

He frowned, staring at her warily with lowered eyebrows.

"I don't know what happened to your father," he said finally. "We never talked about your family."

She stared at him in shock. "Never? In all the time we were together?"

He shook his head.

"How is that possible?"

"We didn't talk about the past," he said shortly.

"Never?"

"No."

"Then…what did we talk about?"

"We didn't talk. We just made love."

A cold trickle went down her back.

They'd never spoken about their pasts?

Their relationship had only been about sex?

The car stopped. Silently, Talos got out of the car and opened her door. Looking up, she saw a very elegant French restaurant in a glossy new building with coldly modern architecture. "This is your idea of a quick breakfast place?"

Talos gave her a smile that didn't meet his eyes. "It was your favorite restaurant in Athens."

Once inside, they were escorted to the best

table, which overlooked the crowded street below. The fancy restaurant was elegant and chilly with sterile air-conditioning. There were many waiters but no other diners.

"It's not very popular in here on a Sunday morning," she ventured.

"I reserved the whole place," he said, sounding bored as he opened the menu.

"Why?"

"I wanted you to be comfortable." He closed the menu. "What would you like?"

With a sigh, she opened her menu. It was written in English and French. This place was entirely too coldly elegant, she thought. Looking out the window with longing, Eve saw locals and tourists thronging a colorful street market.

Outside in the hot Greek sun, she saw people smiling at each other, eating at outdoor cafés, bartering good-naturedly in the flea market.

The waiter came and took their order, speaking flawless English with a slightly British accent. After he departed, a different waiter brought them drinks. She took a sip of orange juice, then leaned forward with her elbows on the table.

"All right, Talos," she said quietly. "Tell me why we're really here."

His eyes were dark as they fixed on her. "This past summer, I almost lost my business," he said in a low voice. "A document was stolen from my penthouse which suggested I might be cheating my stockholders of a great deal of money. Of course, I wasn't. But it cast the company's finances in a sordid light."

She stared up at him, shocked. "That's terrible! Did you find out who did it?"

He looked at her, his eyes glittering. "Yes."

"I hope you put them in jail!"

He took a sip of black coffee. "That's not my style."

"But what does that have to do with me—and this restaurant?"

"This is the last place I ever saw you, Eve. Before your accident."

She frowned, shaking her head. "Right before I left for my stepfather's funeral?"

"You left me long before that. Almost three months ago."

"I don't understand."

"Do you recognize this table?"

She looked down at it. "No. Should I?"

"The last time I saw you, you were sitting here with Jake Skinner. Having breakfast with him, just hours after I'd made love to you."

"What?" she gasped.

His hands clenched on the white linen tablecloth. "Kefalas was following you—"

"Following me?" she gasped.

"*Protecting* you," he corrected. "During the one day I had an unbreakable appointment. He phoned me and I dropped everything. I rushed here like a fool to demand an explanation. You tried to laugh it off as nothing."

She thought of the American tycoon whom she'd met at the party. "So that's why you wanted me to dance with him," she said quietly. "To trick me?"

"I wanted to make you remember betraying me."

She shook his head. "I don't!"

"You disappeared from the city. The next morning, I woke to discover my company's name splashed across the newspapers, and my phone ringing incessantly with calls from press and angry stockholders. Skinner gave the document to the press. But the one who first stole it from my house—" he leaned forward, his eyes black and hard "—was you."

She drew back in shock. "Me!"

"And so I've been waiting for you to remember. Every place I've taken you, every memory I've hoped to reignite, was so you could tell me why."

Suddenly, she understood everything.

"Not just that," she whispered. "You wanted to punish me. It's what you've wanted since the day you found me in London. You wanted revenge—"

"Justice," he corrected coldly.

"But when you found out I was pregnant, that changed everything, didn't it?" She gave a choked laugh, then covered her mouth with an intake of breath. "You felt you had to marry me because I was pregnant with your baby. You never loved me. All you wanted—was to hurt me."

"I spent months trying to find you before you resurfaced at your stepfather's funeral. You're a wealthy woman, Eve, so you couldn't have betrayed me for money. So you must have done it for love. You're in love with Jake Skinner. It's the only explanation."

She thought of the playboy with his bleached-white smile and shook her head. "I could never love him."

"Then why? Why would you do it? What did I ever do to you?"

She took a deep breath as tears filled her eyes.

"I don't know," she whispered.

"Was it out of spite? Did I offend one of your friends? Did I ignore you or hurt someone you cared about? Why? Why would you give me your virginity—then betray me?"

"I don't know." She took a deep breath. "But…I'm sorry."

He stared at her, his handsome face the picture of shock.

"Just like that?" he whispered. "You admit your guilt?"

"I don't remember this restaurant. I don't remember betraying you. I can't even imagine doing something so horrible." Her eyes filled with tears and she blinked rapidly. "But I knew you had some reason to hate me. If you say I betrayed you, then I believe you. I must have done it." She shook her head. "I don't know why and can't offer any excuse. Except to tell you that I'm sorry, desperately sorry."

Talos just stared at her, wide-eyed, not moving.

No wonder he'd been so cold and distant after their marriage. No wonder he'd wanted to punish her. He'd hated her, but he'd felt he had no choice but to marry her because of the baby.

How would she feel in his place, forced to marry the lover who'd once betrayed her? Her heart ached just to think of it.

"You must hate me," she said softly.

His jaw tightened.

"No," he said in a low voice. "You're not the one I hate."

"Then—who?"

He turned away. "I thought you would remember Skinner if you saw him. I was sure you'd remember loving him."

"*Him?* No!" She shook her head fiercely. "If you say I betrayed you, then I believe you. But not for that man, no. Never!"

She saw the surprise in his face, the dawn of insecurity. "How can you be so sure?"

"He's dreadful!"

"Perhaps you didn't always think so. You've changed since the accident, Eve."

She bit her lip, looking down at her pink cotton tank top and simple beige skirt. She suggested in a small voice, "I was more attractive to you before?"

Unexpectedly, he reached his hand over the table, placing it over hers.

"No," he said in a low voice. "You were selfish and cold then, only focused on yourself. Now…" He took a deep breath. "You're different. You care about other people. You're loving and kind and sexy as hell. I've tried not to want you, Eve. Tried not to care. I've tried. And failed."

Her heart was in her throat as she looked up at him, tears in her eyes. She took a deep breath.

"I love you, Talos," she whispered. "Whatever I felt for you last summer—I'm in love with you now."

His hand trembled over hers. He started to pull his hand away, but she stopped him, pressing his hand to her cheek.

"And I'm sorry," she whispered into his skin, pressing her lips against the back of his hand. "Forgive me."

She felt his hand shake, but instead of pulling away, he suddenly took one of her hands in both his own. Looking up, she was startled to see the weight of emotion shimmering in his eyes.

Clearing his throat, he glanced around at the elegant, empty restaurant. "Let's go have breakfast somewhere else."

Looking into his face, she felt her heart leap in her chest. Suddenly, she knew everything was going to be all right.

She now knew the reason he'd treated her so badly—but now he'd finally told her the truth, it could be healed. He could forgive her. She wouldn't stop trying until he did—and until she remembered why she'd done it. And they could be a family.

Wiping tears from her eyes, she nodded.

Still holding her hand, he threw a large wad of bills on the table, then took her out into the bright sunshine.

The Greek sun was already starting to burn white. But as they crossed the busy street, the morning was fresh and new to Eve. Joy was everywhere.

Talos held her hand tightly as he led her

through the traffic, protecting her body with his own. They hurried past ancient white stone buildings packed between new trinket shops. She saw young mothers playing with their children on balconies draped with clothes hanging out in the sun to dry, wizened grandfathers smoking as they played chess in the sun.

Palm trees waved above them, providing respite from the early heat as they crossed into the Plateía Avissynías, an outdoor bazaar rich with music, the sizzle and smell of souvlaki and loud, boisterous haggling in the market stalls over everything from jewelry to Turkish carpets.

And Eve suddenly knew happiness was waiting for them around every corner.

"I'm sorry I wiped out your fortune," she said once they reached the square. Talos stared at her in surprise.

Then he pulled her into his arms with a sudden boyish grin. It made him so handsome it took her breath away.

"You *tried* to ruin me," he pointed out. "But in the end, the press attention only revealed our integrity. My company is worth more now than ever."

"So really," she teased, "you should thank me."

On the sidewalk, he pulled her closer, his body hard against her own. Suddenly all the traffic and other people faded away.

His eyes were dark. Hungry. He pulled her close, stroking her face upward. "Thank you."

And as he lowered his mouth to hers, kissing her so deeply and purely, she knew she would love him—forever.

Nothing had changed.

And yet everything had changed.

As Talos looked down at her beautiful face in the busy outdoor market, her eyes were still closed. Her lips were swollen and bruised from his kiss.

As he lowered his head to kiss her again, he dimly heard his cell phone ringing from his pocket. He retrieved it and glanced down at it, cursing softly when he saw it was his assistant, no doubt calling about the Sydney deal. "Excuse me," he said with real regret. "I have to take this call."

Her beautiful eyes smiled up at him. Accepting him, flaws and all. Asking only that he accept her, as well.

She'd taken blame.

She loved him. How was it possible?

"That's all right," she breathed. "I'll just—um—look around the market until you're done."

"Stay where Kefalas can see you."

She bit her pink, bruised lip, and he could tell she didn't like the intrusion of a bodyguard, even from a distance. For a moment Talos was tempted to ignore his assistant's phone call, forget the billion-dollar deal and offer to be her own private bodyguard. Then she sighed. "All right."

Talos watched as she wandered toward the market. Even in the loose cotton skirt, he admired her backside. He admired her dark glossy hair, her perfect natural beauty. Her sweetly innocent love for him.

I love you, Talos. Whatever I felt for you last summer—I'm in love with you now.

The phone's incessant ringing finally penetrated his consciousness, forcing him to answer. "Xenakis."

"The Sydney deal is as good as done," his first assistant crowed happily. "Their board just voted in favor of the sale."

"Good," he said, but he wasn't really paying attention. He was watching his beautiful wife walk across the market, looking so happy, so interested in the world around her. He was about to hang up.

Then he suddenly paused. "Have Mick Barr investigate Eve."

His assistant's voice was too well-trained to register surprise. "Investigate Mrs. Xenakis?"

"Have him find out how her father died. See if there's any reason it might be tied to me."

As Talos hung up the phone, his gaze lingered on Eve, so beautiful and natural in the pink tank top and short cotton skirt. Instead of stiletto heels, she was exploring this city—exploring her life—in sandals that were clearly made for walking. Her bright, happy face, once so pale, was starting to tan in the sun.

He'd once thought to use her amnesia against her. He'd never imagined that her innocence and warmth would affect him like this. He felt knocked off-kilter by her tenderness, by her love.

I'm sorry. Forgive me.

He was blown away by her openness and vulnerability. She'd accepted blame for a betrayal she could not even remember. She'd chosen to believe him. To trust him, when all he'd done was lie to her, trick her, punish her. It was enough to bring any man to his knees.

Talos started to walk toward her, but he'd gone only a few steps before the phone in his hand rang. He saw his lead investigator's number and answered. "That was fast."

"I can tell you about your wife's father right now, Mr. Xenakis." Barr paused. "Does the name *Dalton Hunter* mean anything to you?"

Talos's entire body went hot, then turned to ice.

He was only dimly aware of the ebb and flow of people around him as his hand clenched around the phone.

"Dalton Hunter?" he repeated in a strangled voice.

"He died in a car accident when she was fourteen. A few months later, her mother remarried—to a wealthy British aristocrat. He adopted her. She took his name."

Talos's heart pounded in his throat. He

saw black birds soaring in the blue sky above the city and for a moment he thought he was going mad.

Dalton Hunter—Eve's father?

"How was I never informed of this?" he bit out.

"We've known about this for months, boss, but you said you didn't want to hear anything about Eve. You just wanted us to find her."

Clenching his jaw, Talos stared at Eve across the market.

"The mother didn't live long, either. She died a few months after she moved the kid to England. Something about heart trouble."

Heart trouble, he thought. *Dalton's wife.*

And he knew just when Bonnie Hunter's heart trouble had started.

"Right," he said. "Thanks for the information."

He closed the phone.

He stared down at his hands, which had tightened into fists. All these months, he'd thought Eve had pursued him out of a mercenary desire for money—or out of love for Jake Skinner. He'd thought she was shallow and cold.

He'd been wrong.

Eve must have planned this since she was a fourteen-year-old girl. Talos thought suddenly of those books he'd seen in her teenaged bedroom in a newly chilling light. *How to Get Your Man.*

Her whole life since her father's death— the whole meaning of her life—had been to get revenge on the man she thought had destroyed her father, ruined her family.

She must have studied the models and actresses Talos had dated. She'd emulated them. It had all been a carefully constructed facade. She'd done it perfectly, down to the last detail. Except for one thing—unlike his other women, she'd always remained emotionally detached.

Now he knew why.

How she must have hated him.

Now, he looked at her across the crowd, watching the brilliance of her smile as she sifted through a selection of hand-knitted baby booties at a stall.

Dalton would have told his daughter that he was innocent. He would have insisted he was the injured party, told her Talos had turned on him for his own gain. Dalton was charming and manipulative. It was how he'd swindled his own shareholders of nearly ten million dollars before an inside source had alerted Talos to the theft.

Would Eve believe him if he told her the truth?

Yes, surely she would forgive him.

He started to walk toward her. Then he stopped.

He would have to tell her the truth about parents she idolized, two people who were both dead. It would break her heart.

And would it even matter? If she ever regained her memory, she would still hate him. It wouldn't matter if he told her the truth. After a lifetime of loving her father, no explanation Talos could give would ever compete with that. And fairly or unfairly, she would hate him for destroying her most cherished memories and beliefs.

If she ever regained her memory, he would lose her.

Completely.

Forever.

It was simple as that.

Talos closed his eyes. The last time he'd seen Dalton Hunter, the man had been drunk when they'd run into each other in a New York hotel. "You've ruined me, you bastard," Dalton had cried out, staggering on his feet. "I taught you everything, saved you from the gutter and this is how you repay me."

"You were stealing from your stockholders," Talos had replied coldly. He'd left the man without guilt, knowing he'd done the right thing. The man had broken the law and now he was getting what he deserved. He hadn't felt guilty. Not even after Dalton had driven his Mercedes into the Hudson River. He'd cheated—and not just his stockholders.

Talos had believed it to be justice.

He'd never thought of the child Dalton had left behind. He'd never checked up on the man's broken-hearted widow.

Talos's first year in America, he'd gone to the Hunters' Massachusetts estate for Thanksgiving dinner. He remembered Bonnie's glow as she kissed Dalton, right before serving the turkey she'd lovingly prepared. Their daughter—Evie—had been just a chubby kid then, reading books and eating apples in a sprawling farmhouse outside Boston.

Eve had changed herself completely since then. But now that she was pregnant and her cheekbones had softened to a more gentle, feminine curve, he could for the first time see the resemblance to the girl she'd been.

Christ, he was the one who'd had amnesia—except it had been by choice.

In the scandal that followed Dalton's death, there must have been no money left. Bonnie Hunter had gone back home to England. Loving Dalton almost to madness, what would it have been like for her to marry John Craig after his death, to get security for her only child?

She died a few months after she moved the kid to England. Something about heart trouble.

Heart trouble?

No! *Thee mou.* He ran his fingers back through his dark hair, suddenly sweating in the cool morning. No one died of a broken heart anymore.

He looked across the market at Eve. No, they just took revenge.

For ten years, she must have molded her character, changing her appearance, remaking her identity to get close to him—all to repay him in kind. She'd attended the charity ball in Venice on his rival's arm just to get his attention. She'd purposefully set out to seduce him, so she could stab him in the heart.

It was a kind of hatred he'd never imagined in his whole life.

And now she was pregnant with his child.

No wonder she'd crashed her car when she'd found out she was pregnant. No wonder her traumatized mind had gone blank. It was like a severely injured person falling into a coma. It was for survival.

He watched her now at the outdoor market, laughing and haggling over two pairs of baby shoes, one pink, the other blue. Her face was beautiful and lit up. With the new feminine fullness of her pregnancy weight, he recognized the girl she'd once been. She looked so alive, so bright and innocent.

All this time, he'd thought this version of Eve was an illusion.

He'd been wrong.

This—*this*—was the real Eve. This was who she would have been if she'd grown up without grief or pain. This was the woman she would have become if Talos hadn't taken everything from her when she was fourteen years old.

Suddenly, he couldn't breathe. The air stifled him. He felt as if he was choking. He yanked off his tie.

If she ever regained her memory…

She would hate not just Talos, she would hate their child.

Eve suddenly turned as if she felt his glance. Their eyes met across the crowd. Joy suffused her expression. Her violet eyes shone with adoration and love, her cheeks were pink as spring roses.

She was the most desirable woman he'd ever known. The perfect lover. The perfect wife. The perfect mother. And at that moment, as Talos stood, he came to a sudden wrenching decision.

Slowly at first, then faster, he crossed the market. Taking Eve into his arms without a word, he kissed her fiercely. She kissed him back, then drew back with a laugh.

"What is it?" Suddenly frowning, she searched his face. "Is something wrong?"

"Not a thing." And he was going to make sure nothing was ever wrong for her again.

He held her tightly against his chest, cradling her as if he would never let her go, pressing a kiss against her hair.

He couldn't lose her. Couldn't bear to lose this precious, bright angel who'd burst into his life like a miracle. He knew he didn't deserve her. But he couldn't let her return to the person she'd been—another bitter, hardened soul in this cold gray world, seeking revenge, seeking payback. Calling it justice.

For the first time in his life, Talos didn't care about justice. Instead, he prayed for mercy.

Where could he take her? Where could he keep her safe, far from anyone who could remind her of the truth? What place could they hide where no old memories could ever ambush them?

Holding her hand tightly in his own, he pulled her away from the market.

"Where are we going?"

"Home," he said suddenly. "I'm taking you home."

"To the penthouse?"

"To Mithridos." He took a deep breath, and a cloud of fear lifted off him. "My island."

To save his family, to save them all, Talos had to pray she'd never remember—anything.

CHAPTER TEN

THE sunlight was bright, almost blinding against the palatial white villa.

Looking between the sky and sea, Eve thought she'd never seen so many shades of blue—turquoise, cobalt, indigo. As she stretched out on the lounge chair beside the infinity pool, the sky seemed to blend with the sea below. Putting down her pregnancy book, she watched the wild surf of the Aegean crash onto the white sands below.

They'd only been here a few hours, but she'd already happily changed into a new yellow floral bikini and pretty, translucent pink cover-up with a loose belt. She now had a closet full of comfortable, pretty clothes, brought here by her very own personal assistant. Curling her toes in pure bliss, she closed her eyes, relishing the feel of warm sunshine on her face and body.

And she wasn't the only one who seemed to like it. Her eyes flew open and she gasped, placing her hands on her gently swelling belly above the top edge of her bikini.

Had she felt…? Was that…?

"Good morning, *koukla mou*."

She looked back to see Talos on the terrace. He was wearing only swim shorts, holding a tray with two glasses of sparkling water and two plates of sandwiches and fruit. She smiled at him, even though she wasn't terribly hungry.

At least not for food.

Talos was so handsome, she thought, with his tanned, muscular chest, his strong forearms and thick legs laced with dark hair. She still didn't quite understand the urgency that had brought them here from Athens, but he'd been so loving and charming, it had been impossible to refuse his need to take her home.

Since they'd arrived at the island that morning, he'd gone out of his way to make her comfortable here. Eve could hardly believe she was now the mistress of Mithridos, his lavish estate. The private Greek island off the coast of Turkey was accessible only by yacht, seaplane or helicopter. The many servants who ran the enormous white villa had already disappeared after having respectfully greeted her as Talos's new bride.

Now, her husband came forward on the terrace, setting down the tray and kissing her softly on her cheeks. "Do you like it?"

As if there were any way she wouldn't like it!

"It's like a dream," she said softly as he sat next to her on the lounge chair, his thighs warm against her legs. "It's a fairy tale. I love it."

"Good." There was something beneath his black eyes, something she couldn't quite read, that exceeded mere domestic satisfaction. He took a long-stemmed rose from the vase on the tray and stroked the soft petals against her sun-warmed skin. As she inhaled the sweet, heady fragrance, he said quietly, "I want you to be happy. I want to raise our children here."

"Children?" She had the sudden image of making a permanent home here, creating a large, happy family, raising children with their father's smile. "How many children?"

"Two?"

"Six?" she countered good-naturedly.

He looked down at her, his dark eyes smiling. "We can compromise. Three."

"All right." She leaned against him with a contented sigh. "I'm so happy here," she confessed. "I never want to leave."

He flashed her a grin. "Then we won't."

"Just what do you have in mind?" she teased. "A honeymoon that never ends?"

He bent to kiss her lightly, tenderly on the lips. "Exactly."

He went to the white granite table, removing the two lunch plates from the tray. He set them out with silverware and linen napkins. He brought the two glasses of sparkling water to the lounge chairs and handed one to her.

He held up his glass. "To the most beautiful woman in the world."

Flushing with pleasure, she clinked the glass against his. "To the most wonderful man in the world," she said softly. "Thank you for telling me the truth. Thank you for forgiving me. Thank you for putting it all behind us and bringing me home."

His dark brows creased, and he looked away. Tilting his head back, he gulped his water down to the very last drop.

Well, it was rather delicious, she thought as she took a sip. Sparkling and refreshing—just like him. Her husband was indeed a long cool drink of clear water beneath the hot sun. She took another sip, her eyes tracing over her husband's handsome physique.

Then she suddenly sat up straight in the lounge chair. With a delighted laugh, she put her hands on her belly. "I think I just felt the baby move!"

"You did?" He placed his hand on her belly over her translucent pink robe. He waited. "I don't feel anything."

"Maybe I was wrong," she said uncertainly. "I'm new at this." She frowned, straining to feel that little thrum that felt like music inside her, like champagne bubbles tickling within her belly. Then she did, and crowed with delight. "Did you feel that?"

"No."

She pulled off the pink cover-up. Pressing his hand against her naked belly, she watched his face as he waited, visibly holding his breath. As if there was nothing more important to him in the world than being with her, than waiting to feel his child move inside her.

Eve's eyes roamed over his handsome face.

Was any woman ever luckier in love?

Except, a voice inside her whispered, *he still hasn't told you he loves you.*

She didn't need to hear the words, she told the voice firmly. His actions showed he cared. Words were cheap. She could do without them.

Couldn't she?

"I still can't feel anything," he said, sticking his bottom lip out with a boyish scowl.

"You will," she said, hiding a laugh. "Although it might be a while. The book I was reading says it might be another month or two before you can feel it from the outside. But I love that you care about our child so much. I love…" *I love you,* she wanted to say, but she choked back the words. She couldn't say them again. Not when he hadn't said the words back to her. "I… I'd love some lunch."

"I exist to satisfy your every desire," he replied with a growl.

She ate all her sandwich and half of his,

laughing with him, loving him. She felt hungry. Happy.

They spent the day kicking in the surf and walking on the sandy bay beneath the villa. Above them, the hills of the small island were rocky and sharp. The sand was hot on their feet, which were then cooled by the swift blue waves.

And every moment, she could feel his dark eyes on her. As the blue waves crashed over their ankles, he kissed her.

His lips were so tender, his kiss so passionate and forceful as he held her.

Holding her breath, she looked up at him through her lashes. The tanned skin of his naked chest gleamed as sea spray trickled down the valleys and hills of his muscular body. The hot Greek sunlight burned down on them as they stood on the edge of the blue waves.

"Don't ever stop kissing me," she begged.

Without warning, he picked her up in his arms, lifting her against his naked chest, skin to skin.

"I intend to spend my whole life kissing you."

He carried her up from the beach as if she

weighed nothing at all, walking back to the villa. He took the stairs two at a time as he whisked her upstairs to the master bedroom overlooking the ocean. Behind her husband's handsome face, she barely noticed the high ceilings, the open balcony doors and the white translucent curtains waving in the hot breeze off the Aegean Sea.

She was shaking with longing, limp with desire. They never even made it to the bed. As they passed the balcony doors with its view of the wide blue sea, he kissed her. She twisted in his arms, wrapping her legs around his waist as the kiss intensified.

Pushing her against the sliding glass door, he slipped off her yellow bikini as her trembling hands pulled off his swim trunks. They kissed each other frantically, their hands touching everywhere, straining desperately to be close. As she kissed his naked skin, caressing his muscular body, she tasted salt and sun and sea.

With a growl, he lowered her to the soft rug. The breeze cooled their skin as the sheer white curtains waved and twisted over their naked bodies. He kissed down the valley between her breasts to her belly, pushing aside her thighs to lick and suck her slick core. She gasped as he spread her wide, swirling his tongue over her taut nub until she thought she'd go mad. She clenched his shoulders, digging her nails into his skin.

With every flicker of his tongue, she grew tighter and hotter, until she was being swallowed up by dark heat. She felt him thrust his tongue inside her and writhed, bucking her hips, knowing she was about to explode, desperate to hold on just one minute longer.

"No," she gasped softly, tugging him upward. "Inside me."

He needed no further invitation. Rolling onto his back, he lifted her above him then lowered her against his shaft. For a moment she couldn't move. He filled her so deeply.

Then he lifted her again with his strong arms. His dark eyes were intense as he forced her to hold his gaze.

"Ride me," he commanded her, and she could do nothing but obey. She gasped with sweet ecstasy as she rocked back and forth against him.

She heard his harsh intake of breath, saw the

stark need on his face as he allowed her—encouraged her—to control the pace. She held him tight, very tight, their bodies locked as one, both of them breathless and sweaty and panting. And with one last thrust, she exploded.

"I love you," she cried out. "I love you!"

"I love you."

Looking up at Eve sharply as she spoke the words, his body wrapped around and inside her, Talos felt embedded so deeply in her soul that he could not deny it any longer. Not even to himself.

I love you.

Making love to her in Athens had been explosive, mind-blowing. But this was more.

Watching her take her pleasure. Watching her beautiful face shine as she rode him, causing such agony for them both—and such explosive pleasure. When he'd heard her gasp out the words, he could hold back no longer, and he poured himself into her with a sharp cry.

Holding her afterward, he realized why this was like nothing he'd ever felt before. He hadn't just been making love to Eve.

He was *in* love with her.

Looking at his beautiful, pregnant wife, his heart lurched in his chest. *He loved her.* She had brought him back to life, made him feel and see things in his life in a totally different light.

He loved her.

He would die if he ever lost her.

And he prayed they would stay here forever, happy, hidden from the world, where he'd never have to be afraid she might remember—

She suddenly screamed in a hoarse voice that had nothing to do with pleasure.

Covering her face, she rolled away from him.

"Eve!" He cradled her back against his naked chest, trying to see her face. When she finally rolled back to face him, her beautiful face was streaked with tears.

"I had another memory." Her voice was like a whimper.

The chill of fear struck through his heart. "What was it?"

She blinked up at him, her lovely eyes the chilling blue of ice. "I remembered stealing the papers from your safe. I gave them to Jake Skinner at that restaurant, just like you said. Then I ran away from Athens and kept running. I never wanted you to find me. I hated you." Her face looked shell-shocked, bewildered, her eyes filling with tears as she pleaded, "Why? Why did I hate you so much?"

His heart rose in his throat. He stared down at her, unable to speak.

"Tell me why I hated you," she cried.

"I…I don't know," he lied, wanting to protect his wife.

Covering her face, she pushed away from him, curling her body into a fetal position.

"It doesn't matter." He forced her to roll back. He looked down at her. "The past doesn't matter. Not anymore. All that matters is the future. Our baby."

Naked, she stared up at him.

"Do you love me, Talos?" she whispered.

He hadn't expected that question.

Yes, he started to say. *I love you.*

But the words got stuck in his throat. He'd never said them before to anyone.

I love you. And I'm terrified I'll lose you.

When he didn't answer, she sucked in her breath. He saw the misery on her face and knew he'd hurt her at the moment she most needed comfort.

"Eve..." he whispered. He leaned forward to kiss her.

Then stopped himself.

He'd thought by bringing her to Mithridos, a place she'd never been before, he could protect her from the memories.

But it hadn't been seeing the sights of Venice or Athens that had made memories return. She'd had her first memory after kissing him on the Rialto Bridge. Immediately after making love to him in Athens with such joy, she'd been crushed by dark memories of her father's death. And now, just as they'd made love a second time, she remembered hating him.

Memories returned after he kissed her.

Memories returned when he made love to her.

That night, he held her in his arms as she cried herself to sleep. He knew it was woefully inadequate, but he was unable to do more. He wanted to make love to her. He wanted to tell her the truth.

He could do neither.

Finally, after she slept, he could take it no more. Rising from the bed, he stared out the open French doors to the terrace, as the warm breeze whirled the curtains. He stared at the full moonlight floating against the black waves of the Aegean, like lost ghosts caught and trapped in dark, invisible webs to the earth.

He'd thought he could keep them safe here, hidden far from the world.

He'd been wrong.

If he wanted to save his family, he could never make love to his wife again. He could never even kiss her. Because if he did, she would remember everything and he would lose her.

Pain racked through Talos, catching at his breath. He gave one last longing look at his naked, pregnant wife sleeping in his bed. He reveled in her sweet beauty, even as his soul anguished over the tearstains on her face. He watched the pink of sunrise creep slowly over the room.

Then, with his hands clenched into fists, he left her to sleep alone.

CHAPTER ELEVEN

How had it all gone so wrong?

A month later, Eve still couldn't understand it. She lived in an amazing Greek villa on a private island. She was married to the handsomest man on earth and expecting his child. She was happy, healthy, living in blissful luxury beneath the Aegean sun as servants waited on her hand and foot.

But for the last month, Talos hadn't touched her. She'd been alone in her marriage. Alone in her life.

She'd never felt so miserable. Though they lived in the same house, they lived separate lives. Talos worked nights in the office, coming to bed only long after she was asleep, or worse—not coming to bed at all, just sleeping on the couch in his office. She spent her days decorating the nursery, organizing the house, taking the helicopter to the nearby island of Kos to visit the doctor.

She'd done everything she could think of to try and regain his interest. She dressed in pretty clothes, like the pink cotton dress she was wearing now. She'd learned to cook his favorite meals. She read newspapers to learn about his interests—basketball and business—trying to please him, to start conversations, to be available when he wanted her.

All in vain.

The problem was that he *didn't* want her.

Since the first day they'd come to the island of Mithridos, when they'd made love so passionately and exquisitely by the balcony overlooking the sea, he hadn't touched her. Hadn't hugged her. Hadn't come up behind her and embraced her, kissing her neck. He hadn't held her or kissed her.

He'd barely even *looked* at her!

After a month of being neglected and avoided, Eve's heart bled like an open wound. She'd outright asked Talos several times why he was ignoring her, asked him if she'd done something to make him angry.

At first, he'd brushed her off with an excuse. Now, he just avoided her completely.

What had she done to make him so angry?

She was almost afraid to ask one more time, because there was simply no further he could withdraw unless he physically left the island. At least as long as he was still in the house she could pretend they still had a marriage, pretend he was just moody or worried about a business deal, pretend their relationship could recover.

But how could they ever recover when he wouldn't talk to her? When he wouldn't touch her?

He was hiding something. Punishing her for something. What? What did he think he couldn't tell her?

She pressed her fingertips against her eyelids. As the hot November sunshine poured in from the wide-open windows, the warm breeze filling the bright breakfast room with the salty tang of the sea, she was choked with despair.

"Good morning, Mrs. Xenakis."

Eve nearly jumped when she heard the housekeeper's heavily accented voice behind her. "Good morning."

The plump older woman set the tray of fruit, eggs, toast and pot of mint tea on the stone table. "Have a lovely breakfast."

Eve had a sudden flashback to the lunch she'd shared with Talos here on the terrace, the first day they'd arrived on the island. Where had it all gone so wrong? What did she need to remember?

"Where is Mr. Xenakis?" she demanded.

"I believe he is in the home office, ma'am. Shall I take him a message?"

Another message he could ignore? Eve shook her head. Staring out at the sea, she took a deep breath. Her last memory hadn't been a pleasant one. She was almost afraid to know what else she had to remember. What else could possibly be worse?

Talos wouldn't tell her. But his silence this last month spoke volumes. She'd done something else. Something he could not, would not forgive.

She had to remember! She had to make herself remember! Or she feared she'd lose him—and their chance of being a family—before her baby was even born.

She turned to the housekeeper. "Is there a

spare computer in the house? With an Internet connection?"

"In the office, Mrs. Xenakis."

Eve licked her lips. "But I would not wish to disturb my husband. Is there another one elsewhere?"

The housekeeper gave a friendly nod. "There's one in my quarters, ma'am. You would be welcome to use it."

"Thank you," she said in relief. Picking up her breakfast plate, she rose to her feet. "Do you mind if I use it now?"

Sitting in the housekeeper's cozy suite ten minutes later, crunching an apple as she looked at the screen, Eve had barely started her search before she heard an angry voice behind her.

"What the hell do you think you're doing?"

Shocked, she swiveled her chair around to face Talos.

"Hi," she said, trying to act cool even as her heart beat faster in her chest. He looked more handsome than ever in his snug black T-shirt and dark jeans. She gave him a trembling smile. "I'm glad to see you."

"Mrs. Papadakis said you were here," he

replied coldly. "You didn't answer my question. What are you doing?"

Her smile faded. "Since my memory still hasn't returned, I thought I would try and give it a kick start by looking up my name online, to see if I can learn—"

"I don't appreciate you sneaking down here."

Sneaking? "I didn't want to bother you in your office," she explained quietly. "The housekeeper was kind enough to allow me to use her computer." When he continued to glower at her, she tossed her head. "How can you accuse me of sneaking in my own house?"

She started to turn back toward the computer screen, but he grabbed her shoulder. His dark eyes looked grim, almost frightening as he said, "Don't."

"Why?" she demanded.

He ground his teeth. "You should be resting, not trying to research a past that doesn't matter. You should be redecorating the nursery, focusing on our future together and staying healthy for the baby."

"Really?" she said evenly. "If you'd shown the slightest interest in me or the baby for the last month, you'd know I finished the nursery a week ago. But you haven't. You've just been avoiding me, like you did after we were first married." She jabbed her thumb toward the computer. "And since you won't talk to me, this is my only option to figure out why!"

"It doesn't matter!" he said harshly. "Just leave it alone!"

"I can't!" she cried. "Not when you won't talk to me, when you don't touch me, when you won't even look at me!"

"I've given you everything any woman could ever want!" He looked down at her fiercely. "Isn't that enough for you? Can't that be enough?"

She shook her head as angry tears rose to her eyes. "I'm in a beautiful villa, I'm expecting a child—but I'm doing it all without you! You've left me here!" she cried. "Why? Why can't you just tell me the reason?"

He started to say something, then stopped. She could see his tension pulse at his neck as he abruptly pulled away from her.

"You are getting yourself upset over nothing. I'm busy with work, nothing more."

"Is it that you don't think I'm attractive anymore?" She shook her head with humiliation and despair. Her voice trembled as she voiced her sudden fear. "Or is there another woman?"

He stared at her, his dark eyes narrowing.

"Is that what you think?" His voice was low, furious. "You think I would betray you that way?"

"What else am I supposed to think, when you—"

"You are the only woman I want," he ground out. "The only woman I will ever want!"

"Then why?" She shook her head. "I don't understand!"

"This last month has nearly killed me," he shouted. "Each day is worse than the last, seeing you right in front of me but knowing I can't have you. It's like falling into hell over and over again!"

"But I'm right here," she whispered. "Why won't you touch me?"

"If I do," he said in a voice so low she almost couldn't hear it, "I will lose you."

That didn't make any sense. Tears fell unheeded down her cheeks.

"Please, Talos." She looked up at him. "I need you."

Their eyes locked, held. She could see the rise and fall of his chest, hear the shudder and rasp of his breath.

Then with an explosive curse, he surrendered.

Sweeping her up in his arms, he kissed her, murmuring words in Greek. His embrace was hot and tender, full of anguished longing and regret as he kissed her.

"Eve, oh, Eve, I can't push you away," he whispered, looking down into her eyes with dark pain and yearning. "Whatever the cost—whatever happens—I can't hurt you anymore."

For a month now, Talos had been in anguish.

Wanting Eve but not being able to have her.

Loving her but not being able to tell her.

He could have lived through his own pain. He could have continued to endure it forever. But it was seeing the pain in his wife's beautiful face that had finally broken his will.

Horror had gone through him when he saw her in front of the computer where he knew she could eventually discover everything. Her tears pleaded for what should have been hers by right—his love and attention.

There was no place remote enough. Nowhere they could hide. No way he could keep her safe, not when by trying to protect her, he himself had caused her such hurt!

And finally he couldn't bear it any longer.

Scooping her up into his arms, he swept her upstairs into their bedroom. He tenderly set her down on their bed, the bed that they should have shared for the last month. She looked up at him, her eyes shining with tears. He could smell the sweet vanilla fragrance of her hair, feel the softness of her skin. He saw her hand shake as she reached up to caress his rough chin.

"Talos…."

Closing his eyes, he placed his hand over her smaller one, turning his face into her caress. He'd yearned for this for so long. For the last four weeks, he'd had to anesthetize himself—with hard exercise, with ouzo, but mostly with work—to try to fight off the constant desire for the woman down the hall, this frustrated desire that was always rising higher and higher until he feared he'd break apart.

Whatever happened, he could no longer

resist her sweetness. He wanted his wife. Needed her. *Loved her.*

He pulled off the soft pink cotton dress with its innocent eyelet lace. Removing his own black T-shirt and jeans, he dropped them to the floor. His eyes greedily drank in the vision of Eve in her translucent white bra and panties.

Looking into her eyes, he finally spoke the words that had long ago been written across his heart.

"I love you, Eve."

She sucked in her breath, her gaze searching his. Wanting to believe. Needing to believe.

Then he kissed her.

Her lips seared him to the core. With every beat of his heart, he loved her. And all he wanted to do was make his vow of a month ago true; he wanted to spend the rest of his life kissing her.

She moved beneath him on the white blanket of the bed. Above him, he could hear the soft whir of the ceiling fan, hear the cry of the morning birds outside, feel the soft breeze against his naked body.

He touched her naked skin, bronzed from so many days spent outside. He stroked her body all over, worshipping her with his fingertips, with his hands, with his mouth. He was hard and aching for her.

"You love me," she repeated in wonder and joy. "You love me?"

"So much," he gasped. "You have my heart forever."

He kissed her forehead, her eyelids, her cheekbones, her mouth. With a groan, he caressed her body, pressing his legs between her thighs.

When he finally pushed himself inside her, he nearly cried out from the force of his pleasure.

He moved inside her slowly, savoring every second and every inch of his possession. Although—was he possessing her? Or was she possessing him?

She gripped his shoulders, throwing her head back, revealing her swanlike throat.

"I love you," he whispered as he pushed inside her again. He saw the light of joy in her eyes, and was astonished to suddenly taste the salt of tears—his own.

He held her tenderly, moving deeply and slowly inside her until he felt her tense. Until he felt her shake.

Whatever happened, he could not stop. Whatever happened, he prayed he could love her always.

Closing his eyes, he thrust into her one last time. He felt her coil around him, heard her gasp.

"I love you," he cried. And as the force of his words slammed through his soul, he threw his head back and poured his seed into her with a shout of pure happiness.

Collapsing back on the bed, he held her tightly. She was his love—his life. He kissed her temple, pressing his hand against her sweaty face. Praying that somehow, they would be happy.

For one second, he thought they could be.

Then he felt her stiffen in his arms.

He felt her hands pushing at him, shoving at him.

"Get away from me!" Rolling away from him on the bed, she leapt to her feet. "Oh my God!"

He looked at his wife, the woman who had

been so joyfully caressing his body just moments before. By the angry, furious, hateful look in her suddenly proud face, he knew his worst nightmare had come true.

Eve no longer had amnesia.

She stood naked in front of him, her dark hair brushing against her tanned skin as she quivered in rage. Her full breasts heaved over the slight curve of his child in her belly with every pant of her breath. Her blue eyes glared at him with such force he was surprised he didn't die instantly from the blunt icy dagger of her hatred.

Eve's beauty was perfect, and now—to him—it was forever unattainable.

He had lost the sweet woman he loved. He'd lost her forever.

When Talos said he loved her, Eve thought she'd die of joy.

After so many months of yearning, she'd finally felt her husband's arms around her and heard him tell her what she'd longed to hear. She'd known happiness she didn't know was possible in mortal life. Then he'd made love to her so tenderly, with such deep, intense passion, her soul had soared to the dizzying heights of heaven.

Then he'd released her, and she'd come crashing down.

Down. Down. Down.

She'd hit the earth without a parachute. Little pieces of her had smashed into dirt and rocks. Her body and soul had shattered into a million pieces.

"You remember," he said quietly.

"Everything," she choked out.

She realized she was naked in front of him. And she'd just let him make love to her. How could she? *How could she?*

Shaking with a repressed sob, she grabbed her silk robe off the back of the bathroom door, wrapping it swiftly around her shoulders and tying the belt tight. She wiped away angry tears from her eyes before she whirled back to face him.

"Was it some kind of sick joke to you? You destroyed my family, then kept me here as some kind of pathetic love slave?"

"No! That's not how it was!" Rising from the bed, he grabbed her by the shoulders, searching her eyes. "You know that's not how it was between us!"

Against her will, memories rushed through her mind. The two of them running together beneath the rain in Venice. Making love against the backdrop of the Acropolis. How he'd looked at her as he kissed her in the surf, their first day on this island. His laughter. His tenderness. His deep dark passion in the night.

Furiously, she pushed the memories away. She wouldn't think about that. She couldn't.

Misery flashed through her, misery so strong it nearly made her stagger. Just moments before in his arms, she'd been so happy. She'd been filled with joy that he loved her. She'd felt she finally had her place in the world—in his arms. As his wife. Carrying his child.

Now, all she felt was loss a thousand times. It was even worse than when she was fourteen, when she'd lost her father, her home and her mother in space of a few months. *Because of him.*

Because she'd failed.

She'd spent the last eleven years plotting to get revenge. To do whatever it took to take him down. Before he could ever hurt anyone again as he'd hurt her.

Instead, she'd betrayed her family's memory. She'd failed everyone she loved.

She'd always promised herself that she would be a better daughter to John Craig as soon as her revenge was complete. Then, in Istanbul, while hiding from Talos's goons, she'd been shocked—horrified—to hear news of his death. Her stepfather had died without knowing how she loved him.

And now it was too late. She swallowed, blinking back tears. A pity she hadn't been driving faster when her hands had slipped on the steering wheel of her Aston Martin. A pity she hadn't crashed into a speeding train instead of the postbox.

She'd wasted eleven years of her life for nothing.

Talos had managed to keep his company in spite of her stolen documents. He'd tricked her into marrying him. And worst of all, she was pregnant with his child.

Her enemy's victory was complete.

She touched her belly in shock. "I can't believe it," she whispered. "Of all the men in the world—to be pregnant by the one I hate the most. The one I swore to destroy."

He winced, then reached for her. "Eve, please—"

"No!" She jerked away from him. "Don't touch me!" She turned away, heading for the door, desperate to get out of the bedroom, away from the soft, mussed sheets that were still warm from the tender passion of their bodies, away from the scent of him that still clung to her. Away from the happiness of the innocent, explosive joy she'd experienced but moments before.

"I don't blame you," he said quietly behind her, causing her to halt. "When I found out you were Dalton's daughter, I already knew I was falling in love with you. So I brought you here to the island." He took a deep breath. "I thought if I kept you safe and hidden from the world, you wouldn't remember. I prayed you never would."

She whirled around with a gasp, the breath suddenly knocked out of her.

"To punish me?" she said, wanting to cry. She lifted her chin. "To claim your victory?"

Talos bowed his head. "To be your husband," he whispered. "To love you for the rest of my life."

His words crept into her soul like mist, whispering echoes of past tenderness and love.

No! She wouldn't let him trick her ever again!

Wiping away her tears angrily, she lifted her chin. "Don't talk to me of *love*," she spat out scornfully. "My father gave you everything, and you ruined him without mercy. For your own gain."

"That's not true!"

"You never named your source. Who was it?"

"I gave my word I wouldn't reveal that," he said quietly.

"Because you forged those documents yourself!" She gave him a last, contemptuous glance. "My father should have left you in the gutters of Athens to die. And that's what I'm doing now. Leaving you—"

He grabbed her shoulders desperately. "He was guilty, Eve. I can only imagine what lies Dalton told you, but he was guilty. He stole almost ten million dollars from his shareholders. When I found out about it, I had no choice. The man deserved justice!"

"Justice!" Gasping, she slapped him across the face. "He deserved your loyalty," she cried, drawing herself up in a fury. "Instead, you betrayed him. You lied!"

"No!"

"After you ruined him, he drank himself to oblivion then crashed his car. My mother's death was slower. She went back to England to marry and make sure I'd be looked after. But within months of marrying my stepfather, she took a whole bottle of pills to bed!"

Releasing her, he stared down at her in shock. "I heard she died of heart trouble."

She gave a scornful laugh. "Heart trouble. My stepfather loved her. He wasn't going to let anyone speak ill of her or of the way she died. So he and Dr. Bartlett cooked that little fiction for the press. She was only thirty-five years old." She narrowed her eyes. "But you're right. She did die of a broken heart. *Because of you.*"

"Eve, I'm sorry," he whispered. "I did what I thought was right. Forgive me—"

"I will never, ever forgive you." She looked

at him, cold and proud. "I never want to see you again."

"You're my wife."

"I'll be filing for divorce as soon as I return to London."

"You're pregnant with my child!"

"I will raise this baby alone."

He gasped, "You can't cut me out of my child's life!"

"My baby will be better off with no father than with a faithless, treacherous bastard like you!" Tears rushed into her eyes, tears she no longer even tried to hide. "Do you think I could ever let myself trust you? Do you think I could ever forgive myself if I did?"

"Your father was the one who betrayed and hurt your family."

"You have no proof of that," she said coldly. "You are the only liar I see. You said you loved me!"

"I do love you!" His voice was ragged, anguished.

"You don't know what love means."

She heard his harsh intake of breath.

"I do now," he said hoarsely. He reached toward her, inches from her cheek, and in spite of everything, her breath quickened as she recalled all the times he'd tenderly stroked her face. "When you lost your memory, you regained your lost innocence and faith. And somehow you made me find mine," he whispered. "Just give me the chance to love you. Test me as you will. Let me prove my love for you."

She thought she saw a shimmer of tears in his eyes.

Talos Xenakis, the scourge of the world—crying?

No. Impossible. It was another of his cruel, selfish games. She thought of how he'd ruthlessly wooed her in Venice, tricking her into marriage with romance and soft words only to punish her the moment they were married. Crossing her arms, she drew herself up stiffly.

"Very well," she said coldly, lifting her chin. "I will let you prove you love me. Give up this child and never contact us again."

He gasped. "Don't make me do it, Eve," he choked out. "Anything but that."

"If you don't do it, you prove you don't love me," she said with satisfaction. She started to turn away.

Without warning, he grabbed her. Pulling her into his embrace, he kissed her. His lips seared her with longing and wistful tenderness. It was a kiss that held the promise of love to last forever.

She trembled. Then even as her knees went weak, a cold sheet of ice came down over her heart.

Savagely, she pushed away from him. "Never touch me again."

Still naked, he clenched his hands, staring at her. When he finally spoke, his voice was low, guttural.

"I will do what you ask," he said thickly. "I will stay away from you and our baby. But only until I find the proof that your father lied." His dark eyes glittered at her. "When I have proof that you cannot deny, I will return. And you will be forced to see the truth."

She tossed her head, folding her arms.

"Then I am well satisfied, because you will never find that proof." Her lip curled as she gave him one last look. "But thank you. You've just given me your word of honor you'll stay away from me and the baby—forever."

CHAPTER TWELVE

FIVE months later, Eve stood alone by her mother's grave.

It was only the first week of March, but already the first blush of early spring had come to Buckinghamshire. The weeping willows were green and gold beside the lake, splashing the season's first color over the graveyard of the old gray church.

In her white goose down coat and green wellies, Eve felt hot and out of breath after crossing the hill from her estate. Not that it was terribly far, but at nine months pregnant, every move was an effort. Even bringing daisies, her mother's favorite flower, to her grave.

Eve glanced at the daffodils poking through the cold earth nearby. Just a few weeks ago, the ground had been covered with snow. How had time fled so fast? Her baby was due any day now.

Her poor, fatherless baby.

It had been such a long lonely winter. During the five months since she'd left Greece, she'd tried to forget Talos. Tried to pretend that her baby's father was a figment of her imagination, the remnant of a bad dream from long ago. But her dreams had insisted otherwise, and in her secluded, drafty mansion, she'd had one hot dream after another to make her sweat and cry out for Talos in her sleep.

She had tried to lose herself in the life she'd left behind, the whirl of social life, of lunch with friends in London and shopping trips to New York. But it had all just depressed her. Those people weren't really her friends—had never been her friends. She saw now that she had deliberately chosen shallow acquaintances, the kind she could keep at a distance. She'd never wanted anyone to really know her. It had been the only way she'd been able to stay focused on her goal of revenge.

Now what was left?

Even though she'd regained her memory, she wasn't the same woman anymore. Nor was she the happy, bright, naive girl she'd been before her memory had returned.

She almost wished she were. Eve closed her eyes, missing the happy, optimistic, loving person she'd been before. That she'd been with *him*. She missed loving him. She even missed hating him.

But it was all over now.

Her eyes swam with tears, causing the spring countryside to smear in her vision like an impressionist painting.

"I'm sorry," she whispered, placing her hand on her mother's gravestone. "I couldn't destroy him like I thought."

She knelt, brushing earth off the gray marble angel before placing half the daisies on her grave. "I'm going to have his baby any day now. And I forced him to promise to stay away from us." She gave a harsh laugh. "I guess I never thought he'd stay so true to his word. Perhaps he's not the liar I thought." She wiped the tears that left cold tracks down her cheeks, chilling beneath the brisk spring wind as she said softly, "What should I do?"

Her mother's grave was silent. Eve heard only the sigh of the wind through the trees as she stared down at the words on the gravestone.

Beloved wife, they said. She glanced at her stepfather's gravestone beside it. *Loving husband.*

Her stepfather had loved Bonnie since they were children. Then she'd met a handsome Yank in Boston who'd swept her off her feet. But John had still loved her—so much he'd taken her back willingly when she was widowed, even adopting her child as his own.

But her mother had never stopped loving Dalton—who had never loved her back with the same devotion.

Were all love affairs like that? One person gave—and the other person took?

No. Her throat suddenly hurt. Sometimes love and passion could be equally joined, like a mutual fire. She'd felt it.

The desire between Eve and Talos had been explosive, matched. She'd been so lucky and she hadn't even known it. For all her adult life, she'd been focused on the wrong thing. On revenge. On regaining a memory that had ultimately caused her nothing but grief.

A bitter laugh stuck in her throat.

She'd pushed away the stepfather who had loved her, spent time with people she didn't care about, learnt about fashion and flirtation and revenge. And for what? What did she have to show for it—for all her lost youth?

Nothing but the graves of the people who'd loved her, some money she hadn't earned and a coming baby who had no father. Nothing but an empty bed and no one to hold her on a cold winter's night.

"I'm sorry, John." She leaned her forehead against her stepfather's gravestone, placing a handful of the first daisies of spring on the earth. "I should have come home for Christmas. For every Christmas. Forgive me."

Hearing a robin's song from the nearby trees, she felt oddly comforted. She rose to her feet, rubbing her aching back and belly as she straightened.

"I'll try to come back soon," she said softly. "To let you both know how we get on."

And with one last silent prayer over those two quiet graves, she started to walk back home.

Home, she thought, looking up at the Craig

estate on the other side of the hill. A funny way to describe this place. The only place she'd ever thought of as home had been her family's old Massachusetts farmhouse.

At least until recently, when every night she dreamed of a villa on a private island in the Mediterranean that was a million shades of white and blue...

She took a deep breath.

With her eyes wide open, she was left in darkness and shadows. She didn't know who she was anymore. She didn't know what to believe in.

She missed her old faith.

She missed *him*.

Eve felt her baby give a hard kick in response to the emotion racing through her. She felt another pain in her lower back as she wiped her tears fiercely. But obviously Talos hadn't missed her. If he had, he would have followed her here, promise or no promise. He wouldn't have stayed away from his wife and unborn child, searching for some stupid proof when their baby was due any day!

Don't make me do it, Eve. She heard the echo of his anguished voice. *Anything but that.*

She felt a sharp pain through her womb. With a gasp, she stumbled across the driveway and up the steps to the side door.

"Is that you, Miss Craig?" the housekeeper called from the kitchen.

Miss Craig. As if her marriage had never happened. As if she'd actually followed through on her ridiculous threat to divorce him. Hearing her maiden name still choked her—even though she was the one who'd insisted on it. "I'm fine."

The plump-cheeked housekeeper came into the foyer with a smile, holding a stack of letters. "I was cleaning out some of your stepfather's things, as you requested. I almost threw this envelope out with the rubbish but then happened to notice it had your name."

"Leave it with me," Eve gasped. Holding the envelope, she sat down on a hard chair in the dining room—afraid if she went for the cushy sofa in the parlor she'd never be able to get up again. Fake labor pains, she tried to tell herself. Braxton-Hicks contractions. But a moment later, as she leaned back into the chair, another pain ripped through her.

She took deep breaths as she'd learned in childbirth class—alone—and tried to control her sudden fear. Every nerve in her body told her that it was time. She was going into labor.

And she didn't want to do it alone.

In spite of everything, she'd somehow thought he would come back for her.

But why would he? she thought savagely. After everything she'd said? He'd been willing to forgive her cold-hearted betrayal last June, but she'd been unable even to consider the possibility that he'd been telling the truth about her father.

Her father…

Gasping, she looked down at the envelope written in her stepfather's hand. She ripped it open.

Dear Evie,
I found this letter among your mother's possessions after she died. I didn't know whether you should ever see it. Sometimes it's best not to know the truth. I will let fate decide. Your mother always loved you, and so did I. God bless you.

There was another smaller envelope inside. She sat up straight, ignoring another sharp contraction as she saw her father's sharp, faded handwriting. It was a love letter, dated the day before her father's embezzlement had been revealed to the press.

Bonnie,
I can't keep lying anymore. I'm leaving you. My secretary wants adventure like I do—like you used to. But don't worry, honey. You and the kiddo will be fine. I've managed to get a chunk of money, the bonus they should have given me over the years. I've left half the money for you.
Dalton

With a gasp, Eve crushed the letter to her chest.

She'd thought her mother had died of a broken heart.

She'd been wrong.

You never named your source. Who was it?

Sadly: *I gave my word I wouldn't reveal that.*

Her mother had betrayed her father. But within months, she'd been smothered by the coldness of her own revenge. It was the same chill that had frozen Eve over the last five months.

Eve had unknowingly modeled her life after her mother's. She'd given up love, selfishly thrown away her baby's chance for a father, for the cold, dead satisfaction of revenge.

Oh my God, what had she done?

Eve cried out as another pain ripped through her. And this time, it really hurt.

"Miss Craig?" The housekeeper suddenly appeared.

"Call me Mrs. Xenakis," Eve cried, rising to her feet. "I want my husband. Please—get me my husband!"

"Are you in labor? I'll call the doctor—I'll get the car around—"

"No," Eve panted, placing her hands on her belly. It couldn't be time, not yet. "We're not going anywhere—not until—he's here!"

She swayed, her knees nearly buckling beneath her as another pain ripped through her. Her baby was about to be born.

Eve looked around the elegant, cold, drafty mansion. She didn't want to be the woman she'd been, buried in the past as her mother had been.

Eve wanted a future. She wanted her baby to grow up happy and secure, in a home full of life and color and joy. She wanted Talos as her baby's father. As her husband.

She wanted to love him.

And she had the choice.

"Please get me the phone," she panted.

"You stay right there," the housekeeper pleaded, running to the nearby phone. She dialed the telephone number Eve gave her, then, after speaking, she held down the receiver. "His assistant says he's unavailable, traveling in Asia."

Unavailable? In Asia?

Talos must have decided he didn't want her, she thought miserably. He was done with her.

"Did you tell him I'm in labor?" she panted.

"Yes, and that you'd like your husband to come to London as soon as possible. Can I do anything more?"

"No," Eve whispered. There was nothing more to be done. Nothing more to be said. If he was in Asia, he'd never make it back to London in time.

Even if he wanted to.

Eve felt like crying.

As the housekeeper ordered the chauffeur to bring around the car, Eve covered her face with her hands. Why had she been so blind? He'd offered her his love with both hands, and she'd pushed it away. Now she was going to have their baby alone. She'd raise their child alone.

For the rest of her life she would be…alone.

And she would die loving him. A man she could never have. Her child would have no father, and it was all her fault. A shaky sob escaped her lips as she suddenly heard a loud noise, crashing, someone shouting.

"Let me in here, damn you, I know she's here!"

The dining room door banged open. She looked up in shock to see Talos, wild-eyed, pushing past the housekeeper into the house. He fell to his knees in front of her.

"I know you said you didn't want me, but if you send me away now—"

"No," she whispered, throwing her arms around his shoulders with a sudden sob. "I'll never send you away again. You're here. I wanted you so badly, and you're here."

Exhaling in a rush, he closed his eyes and held her tightly. Her voice was muffled against his shirt as she said, "Your assistant said you were traveling in Asia."

"On my way here. I finally tracked down your father's old secretary to a convent in India. I have the proof that you—"

"I don't need that anymore," she said, and she gripped his hand as another contraction ripped through her. "All the proof I need is in your face. You're here. You came. Please," she panted, "never—leave me again."

"I never will leave you," he vowed, his dark eyes shining with tears.

She gasped, arching her back as another pain went through her.

"Oh my God, Eve," he breathed. "You're in labor."

He leapt to his feet, shouting for help. "Kefalas, get the car! My wife is in labor!"

Talos drove her to London, exceeding all speed records to reach the private hospital in time. They were too late for anesthesia. She'd just barely settled into her private suite, and Dr. Bartlett had just rushed in to check on her, before their baby was born.

Talos held her close as their son came into the world, protecting them. And in the instant their newborn baby was placed in her exhausted arms, both their lives changed forever.

Talos kissed his wife's sweaty forehead, then tenderly cradled them both in his arms. Their love was newly reborn in that single instant, brilliant and flashing like a comet illuminating the dark night, shining like a star that would always last.

EPILOGUE

"THEY'RE here!"

Four-year-old John was running up and down the hallways, screaming like a banshee when he heard the helicopter land on the other side of Mithridos. Eve smiled down at her son, even as she tried helplessly to hush him before he woke his two-year-old sister, who always got into everything when she was awake, or his six-month-old baby brother, who generally just sat on the floor and watched it all with his mouth open, drooling from his first tooth.

She'd meant to get dressed before the first guests arrived at their island, but she'd been so busy with the children that time had slipped away from her. Now, she realized to her horror that she was still wearing her white fluffy robe from the shower she'd taken twenty minutes ago. Pausing in the hallway, she glanced into the doorway of her bedroom.

Her ladylike party dress, white with delicate pink roses and twisting green leaves, a sweetheart neckline and a full skirt, was lying across the bed in wait for her.

As she stepped into the bedroom, she felt Talos come behind her, kissing her neck as he wrapped his strong arms around her waist.

"Are you ready for this?" he teased.

She turned around in his embrace, standing on her tiptoes to kiss his mouth. He hadn't dressed for the party yet, either. She was equal parts amused and exasperated to see he hadn't changed. He was still dressed in the casual clothes he had worn to take the children to the beach, shorts and a snug white T-shirt that revealed his muscular chest and legs and that always made her want to devour him whole.

Not a bad idea, surely, on their anniversary...?

She paused, looking up at him, her arms still around his neck. She saw the expression on his face suddenly change. With a wicked smile, he started to lower his mouth toward hers.

Then she heard little John knock something over downstairs, heard Annie cry, heard the baby start to wail as he was woken prematurely from his nap.

With a laugh, she gave her husband a wry look. "And our guests will arrive in about six minutes."

His dark eyes gleamed at her. "So we have six minutes?"

"Talos!" she said with a laugh, knowing what he was thinking. "We should welcome our guests to our home!"

"The kids are downstairs," he growled. "They can do it."

"You're incorrigible!" But still, she sighed with pleasure as he lowered his head to kiss her. They had a chaotic, crazy, artistic life full of friends and children and laughter, bright with color and warm with love. Exhausting, but oh, so happy. It was the life Eve had always dreamed of. Even on five hours sleep a night, she felt grateful every morning. She was lucky. *Blessed.*

After only one kiss, Talos drew back from her, his dark eyes twinkling. "I have a present for you. I wanted you to open it before the Navarres get here and the chaos really starts."

"For our anniversary?" she said in surprise. She looked around the beautiful bedroom, with its enormous bed where they made love every night, overlooking their private island and the wide blue sea. Every inch of the villa had already all been decorated with white lilies and orange roses for their party. Their home had never looked more lush and gorgeous. And Talos's four jets were flying in friends and family from all around the world to celebrate with a three-day, child-friendly party that was costing more than she liked to think about. "You've already given me so much. I couldn't possibly want more."

"Too bad. Open it."

He handed her a black velvet box. She opened it with an intake of breath. Inside, she saw a beautiful diamond necklace with six hanging emerald-cut diamonds, each as big as her fingertip.

"Lovely," she breathed, then looked up with chagrin. "But I didn't get you anything!"

He lifted his eyebrow with a wicked grin. "That's what you think." He slowly stroked her earlobe to her chin, making her shiver. Clasping the diamond strand around her neck, he ran his hands over the six large diamonds, caressing the warmth of her bare collarbone. "This necklace represents our family. One diamond for each of our six children."

"Six?" She frowned. "Have you been glugging ouzo? We have *three* children."

With a dark gleam in his eyes, he lowered his head to kiss her, whispering, "So far."

When the Navarre family came through the front door ten minutes later, they found only children to greet them, cheering and wiggling happily as the dog barked and danced around them amid a profusion of knocked-over flower arrangements. Fragrant orange petals floated softly down through the air.

"They'll be down in just a minute," the nanny told them nervously.

But Lia and Roark glanced at each other and smiled.

They didn't need any explanation.

* * * * *

*Harlequin Presents® is thrilled to
introduce a sexy new duet,*
HOT BED OF SCANDAL,
by Kelly Hunter!
Read on for a sneak peek of the first book
EXPOSED:
MISBEHAVING WITH THE MAGNATE.

'I'M ATTRACTED to you and don't see why I should deny it. Our kiss in the garden suggests you're not exactly indifferent to me. The solution seems fairly straightforward.'

'You want me to become the comte's convenient mistress?'

'I'm not a comte,' Luc said. 'All I have is the castle.'

'All right, the billionaire's preferred plaything, then.'

'I'm not a billionaire, either. Yet.' His lazy smile warned her it was on his to-do list. 'No, I want you to become my outrageously beautiful, independently wealthy lover.'

'Isn't that the same option?'

'No, you might have noticed that the wording's a little different.'

'They're just words, Luc. The outcome's the same.'

'It's an attitude thing.' He looked at her, his smile crookedly charming. 'So what do you say?'

To an affair with the likes of Luc Duvalier? 'I say it's dangerous. For both of us.'

Luc's eyes gleamed. 'There is that.'

'Not to mention insane.'

'Quite possibly. Was that a yes?'

Gabrielle really didn't know what to say. 'So how do we start this thing? If I were to agree to it. Which I haven't.' Yet.

'We start with dinner. Tonight. No expectations beyond a pleasant evening with fine food, fine wine and good company. And we see what happens.'

'I don't know,' she said, reaching for her coffee. 'It seems a little…'

'Straightforward?' he suggested. 'Civilized?'

'For us, yes,' she murmured. 'Where would we eat? Somewhere public or in private?'

'Somewhere public,' he said firmly. 'The restaurant I'm thinking of is a fine one—excellent food, small premises and always busy. A man might take his lover there if he was trying to keep his hands off her.'

'Would I meet you there?' she said.

'I will, of course, collect you,' he said, playing the autocrat and playing it well. 'Shall I meet you there,' he murmured in disbelief. 'What kind of question is that?'

'Says the new generation Frenchman,' she countered. 'Liberated, egalitarian, nonsexist…'

'Helpful, attentive, chivalrous…' he added with a reckless smile. 'And very beddable.'

He was that.

'All right,' she said. 'I'll give you the day—and tonight—to prove that a civilized, pleasurable and manageable affair wouldn't be beyond us. If you can prove this to my satisfaction, I'll make love with you. If this gets out of hand, however…'

'Yes?' he said silkily. 'What do you suggest?'

Gabrielle leaned forward, elbows on the table. Luc leaned forward, too. 'Well, I don't know about you,' she murmured, 'but I'm a clever, outrageously beautiful, independently wealthy woman. I plan to run.'

This sparky story is full of passion,
wit and scandal
and will leave you wanting more!
Look for
EXPOSED:
MISBEHAVING WITH THE MAGNATE
Available March 2010

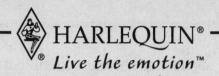

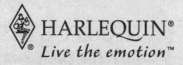

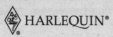

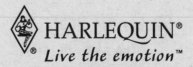

HARLEQUIN®
INTRIGUE®
BREATHTAKING ROMANTIC SUSPENSE

Shared dangers and passions lead to electrifying romance and heart-stopping suspense!

Every month, you'll meet six new heroes who are guaranteed to make your spine tingle and your pulse pound. With them you'll enter into the exciting world of Harlequin Intrigue— where your life is on the line and so is your heart!

THAT'S INTRIGUE—
ROMANTIC SUSPENSE
AT ITS BEST!

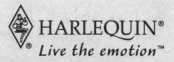

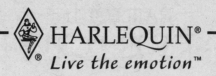

Harlequin® Historical
Historical Romantic Adventure!

Imagine a time of chivalrous knights and unconventional ladies, roguish rakes and impetuous heiresses, rugged cowboys and spirited frontierswomen— these rich and vivid tales will capture your imagination!

Harlequin Historical . . . they're too good to miss!

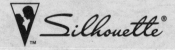